DISNEP

THE MOUSE WATCH

IN SPACE

Disney

THE MOUSE WATCH

IN SPACE

J. J. GILBERT

Disney • HYPERION   LOS ANGELES NEW YORK

First Edition, November 2021
10 9 8 7 6 5 4 3 2 1
FAC-021131-21260
Printed in the United States of America

This book is set in 12-point Goudy Old Style/MT; Nexa Slab/Fontspring
Designed by Joann Hill

Library of Congress Cataloging-in-Publication Data
Names: Gilbert, J. J. (Animator), author.
Title: The Mouse Watch in space / by J. J. Gilbert.
Description: First edition. • Los Angeles ; New York : Disney-Hyperion, 2021. • Series: The Mouse Watch ; book 3 • Audience: Ages 8–12. • Audience: Grades 4–6. • Summary: When their mission to space is hijacked, Mouse Watch agents Bernie and Jarvis must return to Earth in time to prevent its total destruction.
Identifiers: LCCN 2021014755 • ISBN 9781368052207 (hardcover) • ISBN 9781368079570 (ebook)
Subjects: CYAC: Adventure and adventurers—Fiction. • Mice—Fiction. • Rats—Fiction. • Extraterrestrial beings—Fiction.
Classification: LCC PZ7.1.G5488 Mn 2021 • DDC [Fic]—dc23
LC record available at https://lccn.loc.gov/2021014755

Reinforced binding
Visit www.DisneyBooks.com

For Alex

FOREWORD

When Bernie Skampersky told me about her latest mission for the Mouse Watch, I admit I was skeptical. It was an adventure of such magnitude that, at first, it was hard to believe.

However, that all changed when she showed me the recent video footage that had been obtained from Mouse Watch HQ. Although the recording was a bit grainy and raw, there was little doubt in my mind that what I was witnessing was absolutely earth-shattering in terms of its historical importance!

As usual, Bernie had been telling the truth.

Ladies and gentlemice, prepare to read the most stunning account I have yet received from my good friend Bernie. You are about to be taken on a journey so incredible, it stretches the very boundaries of imagination.

After carefully recording every word of Bernie's unbelievable adventure, I found myself, for the first time, craving a bit of adventure of my own. As a mouse author, I am often confined to my hole and prefer the comforts of my pen, paper, and fireplace instead of dangerous missions to outer space.

But that all changes after today. Yes, dear reader, for the first time I, J. J. Gilbert, will pack my suitcases and embark on a secret adventure. I am determined to make it worth writing about, so that one day I, too, may share tales of my courageous exploits with my grandchildren. The voyage will be epic! I don't know when I'll return. . . .

Oh, crumb nuggets. As I'm writing this, I just remembered that I can't leave today. I was planning on sampling a hazelnut honey cake I bought from Mrs. Furrynose's bakery this morning and wouldn't want it to get stale. Oh, and I also really must finish reading that five-volume set of *Historical Mice of Great Importance*. I'm only halfway through volume one. Oh, and there's more cleaning and laundry to do. Not to mention, I really should respond to all the letters I've received from readers asking for more information on the Mouse Watch.

Perhaps tomorrow . . .

—J. J. Gilbert

CHAPTER 1

"Top secret? Isn't everything we do here considered top secret?" Bernie Skampersky asked.

The little mouse's haystack of blue-dyed hair flew back over her head as she hurried past a row of glass enclosed cubicles in the sprawling, high-tech Mouse Watch facility. Her best friend, Jarvis, loped alongside her, huffing and puffing as he tried to keep pace.

They passed a glass-enclosed office with a row of harried looking agents holding digital tablets. The hipster techies were punching away at virtual keyboards and arguing about the best encryption software. Bernie knew that security at Mouse Watch HQ had long been a priority for the organization. The foul rodents of R.A.T.S. were always looking for a way to hack into their databases and servers.

It seemed like whatever the Mouse Watch did to make

the world a safer place, there was an enemy trying to undo it.

Just part of the job, Bernie reminded herself.

The twisting hallways were brightly lit with LED lights that dimmed behind them as the agents dashed down the hall. When Bernie was a new recruit, it seemed to take her forever to get anywhere—the curved halls wound through the building in a dizzying pattern that often confused her. But now that she was a Level Two agent, she was a solid pro and knew exactly, right down to the second, how much time it would take to get to Conference Room A.

"Bernie, (huff, huff) this is an ALL HANDS meeting," Jarvis said, trying to catch his breath. "In all the time . . . that we've been here . . . that's never, (puff) happened."

"That's true," admitted Bernie as she zipped around a drone station filled with flying surveillance robots. "We've got over a thousand agents now! How are they going to pack everybody into one room?"

Jarvis's mop of blond hair flopped comically from beneath his hoodie as he ran, sweat pouring down his forehead. "Hold on a sec, Bernie, would ya? Why do you always want to run? I have a cramp."

Jarvis leaned against a desk, gasping. Bernie danced impatiently in place, glancing at the countdown timer on her smartwatch. She was anxious to get to the meeting. Her black Level Two agent's jumpsuit was sleek and cool. Her smart goggles and watch were activated, and both of them glowed with a steady blue light. When the little mouse caught sight of her reflection in one of the glass walls, she liked what she saw. All her working out was paying off. Her speed had increased so much that having a last name like Skampersky finally did her justice.

She was becoming every bit the Mouse Watch agent she'd dreamed of becoming since she was little.

"Just like Gadget," she murmured happily. Gadget Hackwrench was her hero and the leader of the Mouse Watch. The aging inventor had been an inspiration to her from the time Bernie first heard about her adventures with the Rescue Rangers as a mouseling. It was a dream come true for Bernie to get to work with the legendary founder of the Watch.

"Hey, Jarvie, I wonder if Chip and Dale will be there. I still can't believe they actually personally assigned us to our last top secret mission."

"Don't remind me! And I certainly hope they're not here," groused Jarvis. "Going back underwater doesn't sound fun to me at all."

"But you said you were okay with it," said Bernie. "After we rescued the Milk Saucer, you said that you were getting over your fear of water."

Jarvis gave her a withering stare. "Being *okay* with

something doesn't mean that I'm itching to do it again any time soon." He mopped his forehead with the back of his hoodie sleeve. "I don't care if I ever set foot in a submarine again."

Bernie thought back to their last adventure, reveling in the danger and excitement that they'd experienced deep under the ocean.

She and Jarvis had been assigned duties on the SS *Cheese Dip*, a top secret submarine. They had raced against the clock to retrieve the Million Kilowatt Generator—nicknamed the Milk Saucer—from a sunken Cold War–era submarine called the SS *Moon*. It was an unlimited power device, a secret weapon, one that had been thought lost to history. The mission had been filled with all kinds of things that she'd imagined a top level Mouse Watch agent would face. She'd seen incredible sea creatures in a stunning underwater setting, visited a mysterious underwater city populated with cats, and had also rescued the most powerful weapon that the Mouse Watch had ever found.

The Milk Saucer could have been used to destroy the entire world if it had fallen into the wrong hands.

But thankfully, Bernie and Jarvis had saved the day.

Bernie grinned, thinking about how she and Jarvis had survived so many things. For a second or two, she hadn't been entirely sure that they would escape that mission with their lives (and tails) intact. But they had, and they'd done it together. Rather than scare her off, the danger had only made Bernie crave the next big adventure.

Bernie glanced at Jarvis, who had caught his breath and was now eating a hunk of cheddar cheese he'd been carrying in his pocket. She watched as he drenched it with Tabasco sauce from a mini bottle he'd been keeping in his other pocket, and took a huge bite.

"Seriously! You're eating again? We've got a meeting to get to!"

Jarvis nodded with his mouth full and said in a garbled voice, "Gotta keep . . . *mmf* . . . my strength up."

A cheery voice from behind them caused Bernie to look up. Among the throngs of mouse agents making their way to the meeting was a tall rat with big green eyes and a snaggletooth that stuck out from below her upper lip. She waved excitedly when she made eye contact with Bernie and rushed over, beaming with excitement.

"Bernie!" The rat threw her arms around Bernie in a crushing hug.

"H-hi, Juno!" squeaked Bernie in reply. No sooner had Juno released her grip on Bernie than she had Jarvis crushed in an equally fierce embrace.

"Hi, Jarvie!" she exclaimed.

"Whoa!" Gulp. "Okay!" Jarvis grunted, choking down his bite of cheese. "I can't believe the nickname Jarvie is sticking. B, you're a bad influence!"

"I think it's cute!" Juno said happily.

"You look great, Juno!" Bernie exclaimed.

Bernie had first met Juno during their last adventure, when the rat had turned on her evil bosses and helped Bernie and Jarvis escape. At that time, she'd been a depressed, ragged-looking thing. But Juno had undergone a complete transformation since defecting from the R.A.T.S. Her eyes sparkled, her fur was neatly brushed and clean, and she wore a bright yellow Level One jumpsuit. The rat had often mentioned how much she loved Bernie's blue hair and had, at Bernie's encouragement, dyed her own a bright electric pink, which she now wore in a spiky, punk-rock style.

After a few months at the Mouse Watch, she was a whole new rat.

"Omigosh, did you guys have any of those AMAZING pancakes they had in the cafeteria this morning? I've never tasted anything so good!" Juno exclaimed.

Bernie gave her a puzzled glance. "They were just normal pancakes. . . ."

"Maybe a little better than average with Tabasco sauce," added Jarvis, waggling his half-empty bottle.

"Are you kidding me? They were delicious! And that dollop of creamy ricotta cheese, pistachios, and honey on the side was unbelievable. My mouth still waters just thinking of it!" said Juno, looking shocked. "You guys don't understand. Back at the R.A.T.S. base we had nothing but gray soup for every meal!"

"Gray soup? What's *gray soup?*" asked Bernie.

Juno made a gagging motion with her paw and said, "Nobody knows. Most of us think it was the dirty water left over from washing old socks in the rusted washing machines."

"EEEWWW," said Bernie and Jarvis in chorus.

"Right!" agreed Juno. She stretched her arms wide, indicating the entire Mouse Watch facility. "This is heaven! I can have baths whenever I want! There's good food, great friends, and nobody ever calls me names. I've never been so happy!"

Bernie felt a surge of compassion for her new friend. Jarvis had told her everything he'd gone through before they met and how hard life could be for rats. But hearing it again from Juno only reminded Bernie how grateful she herself should be.

A chime sounded on Bernie's smartwatch. Looking down, she saw the running, cartoon version of herself, and next to it, a text that read, *MEETING BEGINS IN TWO MINUTES.*

"Guys, we gotta hurry!" said Bernie.

"Why is everything *hurry* with you these days?" grumbled Jarvis. "Whatever happened to leisurely walks? Or, better yet, getting electric scooters that can take walking out of the equation entirely! I need to mention that idea to Gadget. . . ."

Bernie and Juno half-dragged, half-pushed a protesting Jarvis the rest of the way to Conference Room A. They ended up being the last to enter with just a few seconds to spare. Once inside, Bernie gazed around. Jarvis was right, it was as big as a stadium! Rows and rows of seats, enough to house the entire California division of the Mouse Watch, stretched from floor to ceiling. The place was practically filled to capacity, and Bernie was glad when Jarvis spotted a row of three seats together near the stage.

As they sat down and settled in for the meeting, Bernie lowered her Mouse Watch goggles so that she could see the stage in enhanced reality. The goggles she wore weren't the standard issue. These were SeaGogs, nicknamed Soggies by the crew that served on the SS *Cheese Dip*. Her original pair, unfortunately, had been stolen by Captain Octavia on the underwater mission, and she wished she still had them.

I won't let her get away with that. Someday, I'll get them back.

Her thoughts of revenge were interrupted as the lights dimmed. A spotlight flared. Then, applause filled the massive room as Gadget Hackwrench appeared from behind a flowing golden curtain. She wore her usual lavender coveralls and her graying hair was cut in a neatly coiffed bob.

Like the other agents, she wore a pair of enhanced reality goggles perched on her forehead.

She waved at the huge crowd with excitement dancing in her eyes.

"Greetings, Watchers!" said Gadget. "Thank you all for coming. I'm excited to say that today is definitely a day we'll all remember. I'm very proud to present what I think is my greatest invention to date." A hush of anticipation filled the room. Bernie could hardly sit still. Her mind raced, thinking about all the incredible things Gadget could make.

I'll bet it's something amazing, she thought. After all, why the big meeting if it wasn't going to be spectacular?

"I'm thinking it's a time machine," whispered Jarvis.

"What?" Bernie hissed back.

"A TIME MACHINE! Wouldn't that be cool?" asked Jarvis. "If I had one, I would go back to the Old West and meet my hero, Tabasco Johnson. He was the gunslinger who invented the sauce that makes life worth living."

"I think that's impossible, even for Gadget. You've been streaming too much sci-fi on MouseTube," said Bernie.

"You can never have too much sci-fi," said Jarvis seriously. "I just completed an amazing series on alien abductions. B, you totally should watch it."

"No, thank you," said Bernie, grimacing. "I hate that stuff. Creeps me out."

"Are you kidding me right now? Science fiction is the best!" Jarvis appeared to be settling in for a debate when Juno elbowed him to be quiet.

Gadget continued her speech. "Ladies and gentlemice, allow me to introduce to you a very special someone. It's someone who can be several places at once. Someone who knows more information than ten thousand encyclopedias and all the professors of all the colleges in the world put together. This someone will be your best friend and the R.A.T.S.' worst enemy. Mouse Watch agents, please give a warm round of applause for . . . *Tony!*"

CHAPTER 2

*H*i, *everybody! I can't tell you how excited I am to be working with you!*

Every jaw in the stadium dropped as a friendly, disembodied voice filled the room. Bernie wondered what was going on. Was there someone hiding backstage with a microphone? *What's the big deal?* she wondered. She glanced around, puzzled at the response.

Gadget noticed all the puzzled looks and chuckled. "No, you won't see Tony walking around. Tony is our new, state-of-the-art artificial intelligence agent that will be helping to *catapult the Mouse Watch into the future!*"

No way! That's so cool!

The voice sounded incredibly real and had a casual tone that was like listening to an old friend who had stopped by for a visit. Bernie had heard AI voices before on smartphones, but this one was very different. Tony actually sounded like a real mouse, and it was hard to believe that the voice didn't have a physical body to go with it.

"That's right, agents, with the help of Tony's vast database, we'll be able to take our mission to save the world to a whole new level!" said Gadget.

Polite applause.

"*Tony* stands for Tailored Omnipresent Nice guY," Gadget continued. She shrugged sheepishly and added, "I know, I know. . . . The acronym is a bit of a stretch using the Y on the end of *guy*. But *Tong* sounded too much like a salad server and he's so much more than that."

Polite giggles.

Gadget, grinning at the crowd, continued her speech. "Tony will customize himself to your personal needs and is there for you when you're in a pinch. He will never let you down."

Scattered applause filled the vast chamber. It was evident that many of the agents were still feeling a bit confused as to what exactly Tony did or where he was. Gadget could see the mystified expressions on a lot of the agent's faces and motioned for silence. "I know it's a lot to take in. The Tony system will be integrated into our new fleet of drones, enabling them to navigate obstacles and make split-second decisions that could save our pilots from danger." Gadget directed her voice skyward. "Hey, Tony, would you mind describing for everyone what sorts of other ways you could help on a mission?"

The Tony program chuckled, and the system's voice echoed around the room as it replied, *Sure thing, Gadg.*

Gadg? thought Bernie. *I've never heard anyone call her that.* Gadget was very nice, but she was also such a great leader. Everyone respected her so much that Bernie couldn't imagine being that informal with her.

Let's see, well, the first thing to know about me is that I never sleep and I don't eat . . . much, Tony joked. A few mice giggled, breaking the stunned silence.

"That's good," whispered Jarvis, grinning. "I don't need the competition."

"Pay attention!" hissed Juno.

Tony continued, saying, *The truth is, I cater my database toward the individual needs of the agent I'm interacting with. You'll find that I'm a friend you can count on and that I'll get to know you better the more you ask me for help. I learn from you and you can learn from me. Isn't that great?*

Gadget nodded and gestured toward the crowd. "Beneath your chairs you'll each find a small case. Please reach down and open them now."

Feeling puzzled but excited, Bernie felt around beneath her chair and pulled out a small, plain-looking black box. She lifted the silver buckle that kept the lid fastened shut.

Then, after opening the top of the case, Bernie's heart skipped a beat.

"New goggles!" she exclaimed happily. These new ones looked so cool, she almost forgot her grudge against Octavia for stealing her old ones. The specs had sweeping black-and-chrome sides and a tiny Mouse Watch logo, the iconic MW gear, engraved between the lenses.

She immediately put the sleek device over her eyes. As soon as the goggles booted up, Tony's voice sounded loud and clear, as if he were sitting directly on her shoulder.

Hi, Bernie Skampersky! Nice to meet you! How are you doing?

By some high-tech wizardry, Gadget had managed to have the AI voice conduct directly from the goggle's contact point at her temple into her head without any kind of special attachment or earpiece.

"Wow!" whispered Bernie, startled at how realistic the effect was. She'd had no idea how the system had recognized her by name, but judging by the gasps of delight around the room, all the other agents were experiencing the same thing.

Well? Cat got your tongue? asked Tony.

"C-c-cat? What cat?" asked Bernie nervously.

Oh, that's right, you've been to Catlantis. Bad joke. Seriously, I've really looked forward to meeting you. I've scanned all your records and I have to say, I am quite *a fan!* said Tony.

Bernie blushed. Although Tony was just a computer program, it sounded so real that she couldn't help feeling flattered by the compliment.

"Um, thanks," said Bernie. "I really don't know what to say. Am I supposed to ask you to do something?"

You can if you want to. Or, if your mind's a blank, I could show you how to work your new goggles. I really think they're the most impressive thing Gadget has ever come up with.

"Now that's saying a lot," whispered Bernie.

I agree! said Tony. *And she also invented me so that's REALLY saying a lot.*

Bernie laughed. Juno, who was sitting on Bernie's left, leaned over. Bernie noticed that she was wearing her goggles and had a look of stunned amazement on her furry face.

"Do we really get to keep these?" Juno asked, awestruck.

Bernie nodded. Juno looked so excited she could have fainted on the spot. "This . . . is . . . the . . . greatest . . . day . . . of . . . my . . . life!" she exclaimed.

Tony's voice sounded in Bernie's ear. *Hey, let me show you something real quick. You'll love it. Okay, so when you think about the best day you've ever had, what comes to mind?*

Bernie's mind flashed back on a particular day she'd spent with Jarvis. "Well, once Jarvis and I had ice cream at this great little shop in Santa Barbara. We took the train up there on a Saturday when we didn't have any Watcher duties—"

Okay, let me stop you right there, interrupted Tony. *Let me check my database. Oh, got it. You had peppermint-candy ice cream, right?*

"Yes! But how could you possibly know that?"

Tony laughed. *I cross-referenced all the ice cream shops in Santa Barbara, found security camera footage of every Saturday in the last year, face mapped every visitor, and found a recording of you and Jarvis. Simple.*

It certainly didn't sound simple to Bernie. Tony was faster than the fastest computer she'd ever used.

Okay now, sit back and close your eyes. Relax.

Bernie automatically did as she was told.

The temperature that day was seventy-four degrees Fahrenheit, Tony said. *There was a light breeze out of the west, carrying with it the scent of the beach and a nearby hot dog cart. . . .*

Bernie felt a warm breeze tickle the fur on her face and arms, carrying with it the delicious scent she remembered. Even though she *knew* she was inside a crowded stadium, she *felt* like she was there, in Santa Barbara, breathing in the fresh air.

"How did you do that?" Bernie asked, amazed.

Never mind. Tony chuckled. *Way too complicated to*

explain advanced neural haptics right now. Okay, you should be feeling a spoon in your right paw right . . . NOW. Do you feel it?

Bernie grinned and nodded as her paw closed around what felt like a plastic spoon. "Wow!"

Okay, Tony whispered. *Now, with your eyes closed, dip that spoon into the peppermint ice cream you imagine sitting right in front of you and take a bite.*

Bernie obeyed. To her utter amazement, she felt the cool, creamy texture of McCornell's peppermint-candy ice cream on her tongue. She swallowed, and it felt like she'd eaten some even though it wasn't there.

"AMAZING!" Bernie cried.

Amazing is what I do, said Tony proudly. *And that's just for fun. Imagine if you needed to process an environment prior to doing a mission? You would know exactly what the conditions felt like and what you were up against.*

Bernie opened her eyes and shook her head in amazement. It seemed like just when she thought she'd seen the best of what Gadget could do, her mentor always surprised her.

The entire stadium filled with a rising commotion of "oohs" and "aahs" as Tony led the other Watchers through similar experiences. After a few seconds, Gadget motioned for silence and all eyes were once again riveted back upon her. This time, every agent in the assembly could see the incredible possibilities for what Gadget had created. The hushed crowd was as attentive as if they were at a magic show and Merlin himself was performing.

"So, as you can see, Tony has many uses," Gadget said. "But the system is just the beginning. Tony is critical to the next phase of Mouse Watch security."

Behind Gadget, a projector flickered on, and a three-dimensional, holographic display of a metal sphere with long antennae coming out of it appeared. It rotated slowly and majestically on the stage.

"Thanks to the recovery of the Milk Saucer by agents Jarvis Slinktail and Bernadette Skampersky, we are about to launch a brand-new, top secret satellite into space." Gadget gestured to the hologram. "The goal of this satellite is to use the Milk Saucer's powerful, endless energy source to save the planet. Ladies and gentlemice, with this new invention we will create a bubble around Earth that will halt, and reverse, the effects of global warming permanently."

Excited gasps filled the room. Bernie could hardly believe her ears! What Gadget was proposing could save millions of lives, many more than the Mouse Watch had ever saved in its entire history! It was staggering! It was stupendous!

"And this mission to space," Gadget continued as

the thunderous applause died down, "will be conducted by none other than our two up-and-coming stars in the Watch. Jarvis Slinktail and Bernadette Skampersky, would you please stand up?"

Bernie thought she had fur in her ears. With stunned looks on both of their faces, she and Jarvis rose shakily to their feet. In a billion years Bernie would have never guessed that this would be happening. She was overwhelmed by the waves of raucous applause that once again erupted across the room.

Gadget grinned and motioned for quiet. "These young agents have impressed us all with their courage and unique talents. I feel certain that they're up to the task of going where no mouse has gone before—outer space."

Another round of cheers echoed through the big auditorium. Juno banged her paws together so hard that her goggles nearly fell off. Bernie's mind was reeling. She saw Jarvis out of the corner of her eye and was shocked to see that rather than wearing the usual sick look of fear that the news of a new mission had produced in the past, he was grinning ecstatically.

"I *knew* watching sci-fi movies would pay off!" he shouted.

Up until that moment, Bernie had believed that there was no danger she wouldn't have loved to face. She'd even been hoping for more! But with the terrifying reality that she was going to be rocketed into space, Bernie felt more than just weak in the knees.

The agents exited the assembly, placing their old goggles into the provided recycling bins and donning their exciting new ones. Bernie's mouth was dry and her paws shook as she endured the steady stream of congratulations, handshakes, and good-natured shoulder squeezes.

"Hey, Bernie, are you okay?" asked Jarvis, noticing for the first time how pale she'd gotten.

Bernie couldn't find the words to reply. For an answer, she ran as fast as she could to the nearest bathroom and completely lost the pancake breakfast that Juno had been raving about just a little while ago.

CHAPTER 3

"That's totally not fair!" said Bernie.

The lanky rat glanced down at his friend and shrugged. "You rolled a one," he said. "It just means that you have below average intelligence. Why are you so upset?"

"Below average!" Bernie spluttered. "A ONE means my character can barely tell the difference between a banana and a smartphone! C'mon, you have to let me roll again. Mouse Elf sorcerers need intelligence! I won't be able to conjure any spells . . ."

Bernie knew that she was more agitated than usual. In the past when she, Jarvis, and Juno had gotten together to play Mice and Dice it had relaxed her. But now, all she could keep thinking about was the upcoming mission, and everything felt stressful.

For the first time in her life, Bernie was terrified. She'd been nervous before, even scared. Back at Catlantis, she'd faced cats, for goodness sake—one of her biggest fears ever. But this . . . nothing compared to this. Going to outer space was something that she'd never thought she'd ever have to do.

"The rules of Mice and Dice are clear," interrupted Jarvis, holding up a paw and assuming a lecturing pose. "Each player has to take the stats they get when they roll a d20. It's in the rule book."

Bernie ran a frustrated paw through her tall wave of blue hair. "I don't care about the rules."

"Well, no surprise there," snorted Jarvis. "What's wrong? Ever since the meeting you've been acting weird."

Bernie didn't want to talk about it. In the past, she had always been the one who'd calmed Jarvis down. She just couldn't stand being the one that was a scaredy mouse. If word got out, what would Gadget think?

"How come you're not wearing your new goggles?" Bernie asked Jarvis, changing the subject. "They're really amazing. I figured you wouldn't be able to stop talking about them."

Jarvis shrugged. "I dunno. Ever since we lost the Wi-Fi during our last mission, I'm kind of becoming less and less attached to tech. I've been reading these weird, little rectangular objects called books." He gestured to the big stack

of Mice and Dice modules. "They're great! And they never need recharging!"

What is going on with the world? thought Bernie. *It's like everything I thought I knew is getting turned upside down. Jarvie isn't into tech anymore, and I'm a total chicken. I feel like I'm having a bad dream!*

Your pulse and breathing have accelerated, said Tony's voice. *What can I do to help?* Bernie flinched, startled by the tech. Now that she'd activated her new goggles, Tony was able to talk to her wherever she was as long as they were with her.

"I'm not nervous," Bernie lied. "I'm just, er, really excited about this game I'm playing."

"Wait, you are?" asked Juno. "You didn't seem excited a second ago."

Bernie realized that, since Juno couldn't hear what Tony was saying in Bernie's ear, her friend was only getting one side of the conversation.

"I am! I'm, like, soooo excited," lied Bernie, grinning with all her teeth and trying to muster up some fake enthusiasm. "But I think there was something that I . . . um . . . ate earlier that didn't sit well. I'd better go lie down."

The look Jarvis gave Juno made it clear that neither of them believed her for a second.

"Ookay," said Jarvis. "Right. Well, I guess we can always fight the Rat Zombies next time."

"I hope you feel better," said Juno. "You've got that big mission coming up, and it would be a shame to miss it."

"Yeah, totally," said Bernie as she quickly stood up from the gaming table and edged toward the door.

"Remember we have space training tomorrow," called Jarvis. "It's gonna be so cool! We're gonna be real astronauts, B! Just think about that!"

"Oh, I'm thinking a lot about it," Bernie said. Then as she left the room, she mumbled to herself, "Seems like I can't get it out of my head."

I can help with that, came Tony's soothing voice. *How about some nice music or a virtual walk on a beach?*

"Thanks, Tony," said Bernie. "But I really don't think it will help."

Instead of dashing about Mouse Watch HQ as she usually liked to do, Bernie shuffled slowly back to her quarters and shut the door. The room was simple and modern, with a comfortable bed and streamlined furniture. In the corner of the room stood the Candroid, a metal, mouse-shaped droid that "*Can* do everything." It had been switched off since Gadget introduced Tony to the Watch and was now an outdated information system. Bernie couldn't stand the thought of the Candroid being recycled and had asked to keep it in her room.

"You were here when I first arrived," said Bernie. She ran her hand affectionately over the robot's large right ear.

She thought about how excited she'd been at that time. She'd felt a little nervous back then, but not terrified like she was now.

"If I could just follow the advice I gave Jarvis when he was scared of the ocean," Bernie muttered. "I told him not to worry, that we'd be okay and I would look out for him." *And that's so much easier to say to yourself when your insides aren't shaking around like a bowl of Jell-O in an earthquake,* she thought.

Bernie flopped down on her bed and covered her face with a pillow. She lay there for a long time, with her mind racing about the training they were supposed to start tomorrow.

In three days, I'll be shooting into the air like a firecracker!

And as soon as she thought of that image, her trembling got even worse. Her paws shook and her heart started racing.

I can't believe I'm doing this, thought Bernie. Her mind flashed back to an early memory, one of being forced to watch *Vampire Rodent Invaders from Planet Z,* a cheesy sci-fi horror movie that she'd seen when she was just a mouseling. Her brother had had some friends over on the Fourth of July when she was four years old, and, although he'd warned her that it might be too scary, she'd wanted to prove she was as brave as they all were.

It turned out she wasn't.

Bernie had dealt with nightmares over that movie for many years afterward. She'd never mentioned it to anyone because she was sure she'd be made fun of. Most mice would have considered the special effects to be low grade and the rubber-suited aliens laughable.

But Bernie's young imagination had run with the movie and she'd been afraid of outer space—and especially the idea of aliens—ever since.

Only recently, in the last couple of years or so, had the nightmares gone away. She'd been sure that she'd finally outgrown her childhood fears, but now that she was actually going up to space, she was certain that the nightmares would come back.

And as crazy as it sounded, what if they turned out to be true?

Bernie gazed up at the ceiling. She turned on a night-light, closed her eyes, and tried to force herself to relax. But she couldn't stop thinking of the skyrockets she'd seen from her little house in Thousand Acorns on that Fourth of July so long ago. They were pretty, but every single one of them always ended with a loud, spectacular BOOM!

If only there was a way to get out of this, she thought as she drifted into an uncomfortable and troubled sleep.

CHAPTER 4

Bernie's sleep that night was filled with dreams of failed rocket launches and explosions, panicked breathing, sweating, moaning, and lots of tossing and turning. Worse still, a few of her nightmarish, slimy aliens made an appearance, too.

She woke up several times during the night, catching herself before she could scream.

Just prior to dawn, she had a final, awful dream. In it, she was lost in space and floating away from an exploded spaceship—drifting, drifting alone in the vast nothingness without anyone to help her. As she flailed her arms in the dream, her gloved paws got entangled with her space suit's breathing tubes, and then the breathing tubes turned into tentacles. An alien wrapped itself in a death grip around her, and just as it raised its fanged mouth to bite her neck, she yelled herself awake.

The next thing she knew, Bernie was gasping for air with all the blankets twisted up around her head and arms.

Bernie lay in bed for a full five minutes, bleary eyed and nervous, trying to catch her breath and clear her head. *There's no way I can do this*, she thought. *I'll just tell Gadget that it's too much. She'll understand, right?*

Bernie would have, at that moment, given just about anything to get out of the mission. But as often happens, as the light of the morning grew brighter, it chased away the shadows of the night before. The nightmares were replaced with the conviction that as much as she wanted to, she really couldn't get out of her assignment.

She needed to be brave. She couldn't let Jarvis down. She couldn't let Gadget down. She couldn't let the world down! Here they were on the cusp of saving millions of human and animal lives and she was letting a little thing like her own fear of slimy aliens get the best of her.

She was an agent of the Mouse Watch! It was time to find a little backbone.

Bernie sighed. Then she forced herself to get showered and dressed. Using her favorite brand of mouse mousse, she sculpted her blue hair into its usual towering wave. Most days, she would have hurried to the Mouse Watch cafeteria for breakfast, but today she didn't feel hungry. She shuffled despondently down the glass-walled corridors, with her hands shoved deep into her jumpsuit pockets, barely acknowledging the greetings of her fellow agents or the scent of blue cheese soufflé and bacon that wafted through the hallways. At one point, a little agent wearing a rocket pack jetted past her, roaring so close she singed the tip of one of Bernie's whiskers. Bernie didn't even notice.

When she finally arrived at the bustling cafeteria, Jarvis and Juno were already finished eating and were waiting to meet her outside the crowded mess hall. Bernie usually loved gazing at the vaulted modern ceilings in the cafeteria and admiring the elegant banners displaying images of many of the great Mouse Watch agents from the past. But today, she didn't even peek inside. Until this morning, Bernie had always wondered if she'd ever be counted among those heroes. But at that moment, she felt like she'd make a mistake even joining the Mouse Watch in the first place. Facing this nightmare had cast her entire future in doubt. She felt she'd be lucky just to make it back alive much less immortalized.

As Bernie drew near to Jarvis and Juno, a round bespectacled mouse named Sylvia Gleamfur held up her paw. At first, Bernie thought she was motioning for her to stop for some reason.

"PPPSSSSHHHOOOEEWWWWWW!" said Sylvia, zooming her paw through the air like a spaceship. When she finished, the round little mouse grinned and pushed her glasses farther up on her snout. "You're tho lucky!" she added with a lisp.

Bernie nodded and managed a weak smile, not feeling lucky at all.

"Er, thanks, Sylvia."

"Nexth time, I'm gonna tell Gadget to pick me," she said enviously, slipping away down the hall after a group of chattering Level Ones.

Bernie felt that she would have gladly traded the position if Gadget would have let her.

"Hey!" said Jarvis, popping the last bite of a gorgonzola muffin into his mouth. "What kept you?"

"Rough night," mumbled Bernie.

"You missed another amazing breakfast," said Juno. "There was a choice of either cheese soufflé or oatmeal! It was hard to pick, so I chose both. Oh, and when I had oatmeal, I got to have it with as many raisins as I wanted! I didn't even have to count them!" She said this last bit as if it were an unimaginable treat.

"That's nice," said Bernie.

An awkward silence descended on the group. After a moment, Jarvis cleared his throat and said to Juno, "Well, Bernie and I should probably head over to Training Room C."

"Good luck, you two!" said Juno. She looked kindly at

Bernie and put a paw on her small shoulder. "You're gonna do great! Don't you worry about a thing. A tough mouse like you can take on the whole galaxy!"

It was a really sweet thing to say. Bernie wanted to thank Juno for her encouragement, but the words just wouldn't come. With her throat feeling tight and a little choky, all she could muster was a quick nod and a tight-lipped, nervous smile. On their way to the training center, she listened to her best friend prattle on and on about the excitement of space.

"Oh! And there's a volcano on Mars that's three times the size of Everest. Can you believe that? Oh! And did you also know that neutron stars are the densest and tiniest stars in the known universe? They've got a massive gravitational pull, over twice as much as Earth!" He pointed at Bernie and grinned. "They're like you—small but mighty!"

Bernie normally loved it when Jarvis called her "small but mighty." It was a little term of affection that always made them feel close. But this time, it just washed right over her. She didn't feel small and mighty in the least at that moment.

Jarvis stopped walking and turned to Bernie with his paws on his hips. "Okay, you're acting really weird. What's up?"

"Nothing," Bernie lied.

"I know you," said Jarvis. "And there's something going on. I've never seen you like this. First you leave the campaign last night when fighting zombies is your favorite. You're not eating and you've always got this weird, tense expression on your face. Talk to me!"

Bernie was too exhausted to resist. She'd barely slept, and keeping her feelings bottled up inside was too hard. With a long sigh, she said, "I'm terrified of going to space, okay? There, I said it."

She crossed her arms and looked up at Jarvis with a defiant expression, as if expecting him to challenge her. He didn't. But a look of surprise washed over his face.

"Okay, whoa. I've never heard you say you were *terrified* of anything before."

Bernie was about to defend herself, but Jarvis held up his paw to stop her.

"I'm not being judgy! If anyone knows what it is to be nervous, it's me. Remember the sub? I was a total wreck!"

"How could I forget?" said Bernie miserably.

Jarvis noticed Bernie's discomfort and reached down to put his paw on her shoulder. "Hey, I understand that feeling better than you know. Why didn't you talk to me about this before?"

Bernie's throat constricted a little, and she found it hard to talk. "I've always been the brave one. I know that. I didn't want you to be disappointed in me."

The last part came out in a rush and, to Bernie's horror, it almost sounded like she was going to cry. She cleared her throat and looked away. Jarvis gave her time to gather her feelings. Then he patted her shoulder and said, "I could never, not in a million, billion years, EVER be disappointed in you. You're the best friend I've ever had."

Bernie smiled up at him. Jarvis looked at her with such a kind expression that she felt dumb for doubting herself. She slumped down against a glass cubicle wall, and Jarvis did the same.

"I always loved the idea of flying. When I was little, I wanted to pilot a drone! But outer space . . . that's different," Bernie said with a shiver. "All that blackness and no air to breathe. Just the thought of being up there was always scary. I mean, at least when you're in a drone you could land somewhere if something went wrong. But if you have a malfunction in space, you might end up floating up there forever!"

Bernie wrung her paws. "It's my worst nightmare. Plus, there's one other thing . . ." Her voice trailed off. She didn't think she could finish the sentence.

"What's that?" asked Jarvis.

"I don't want to say."

"Come on, you have to now. What's the other thing?"

Bernie hesitated. Then, with a voice barely above a whisper, she said,

"Aliens."

"What?" asked Jarvis, looking stunned.

"Aliens. ALIENS, OKAY?" Bernie shouted. "I saw a really scary movie about them when I was little, and I've been terrified of them ever since. I used to make tinfoil hats when I was a mouseling to keep them away."

Jarvis stared at her. Bernie knew she was sounding unhinged, but she couldn't help telling him about it even if it seemed dumb. "I've had recurring nightmares about this *thing* . . . it has tentacles and a big yellow eye. It can also shape-shift and take over people's bodies."

"Take over their bodies?" asked Jarvis.

"Take . . . over . . . their . . . bodies," Bernie said pointedly. "It's from a movie I watched when I was little. I wasn't allowed to watch it, but my parents had gone to bed and they'd left the iPhone out for my brother and his friends, so . . ."

"Okay, wait. Hang on . . ." Jarvis put a paw to his temple, trying to process what he was hearing. "So, you're afraid of aliens."

Bernie nodded miserably.

"But how do you know if they're even real?" asked Jarvis.

"I don't. But they could be. Nobody knows! They could be out there!" Bernie gesticulated wildly at the ceiling.

Jarvis glanced up and chuckled.

"Don't laugh!"

This section of HQ was less crowded than the area near the cafeteria. Towering glass windows were installed on either side of the walkway, allowing panoramic views of the main command center below. Bernie stared down at several agents boarding the zoom chutes of a Habitrail-style vacuum transportation system that sent agents flying back and forth to the more remote parts of the base. Usually, this sight always brought a smile to her furry face, but she was feeling anxious and embarrassed. She knew how silly her phobia of aliens sounded when she said it aloud, but the fear was real and she hated having to admit it in front of her best friend.

"Okay, sorry. But, I just never thought . . ." Jarvis said and then sighed. "Well, who am I to judge? I have fears of things other rodents don't understand, so I have no right to make fun of you. I wasn't trying to, anyway," he said kindly. "It's just that, well, suppose you did meet an alien. How do you know that they're evil and that they would do something bad to you?"

Bernie thought about that a minute. "How do you know they're not and they wouldn't?" she asked. "Look, I can face almost anything that I can see and touch. You've seen me. You know."

Jarvis nodded.

"But the stuff that really gets me are the things we don't know, and that includes aliens," she confessed.

Jarvis stared at her for a long moment.

"What?" demanded Bernie. Her tail was sticking out stiff as a knitting needle, a sign that she was extremely upset.

"Nothing! I was just thinking that it's so strange that on this topic we could be so opposite. I've dreamed of going to space ever since I was a baby rat. And the thought of meeting a real alien would be super exciting!" He scratched his furry cheek, thinking. "But what you're saying makes total sense to me when you put it that way. I guess because I've played too many video games, I can only see the fun in it."

He gave Bernie a serious look. "The most important thing to know is that you don't have to do this. Bernie, you've done so many amazing things for the Watch, Gadget would totally understand and wouldn't think any less of you. I can tell her we're not going and that she should pick two other agents for the job."

Bernie felt a surge of affection for her friend. The fact that Jarvis was willing to give up his childhood dream for her meant so much. But as soon as he'd said it, she knew what her answer had to be.

"No, Jar. I . . . I'd never make you do that. It means the world to me that you'd offer, but I need to do this. As scary as it is, I have to find the courage to face it." Bernie took a deep, relaxing breath, stood, and then they resumed walking. "But thanks for the encouragement. It helps."

"Always," said Jarvis with a nod.

CHAPTER 5

They arrived at the training section of HQ a few minutes later. As they approached the big, sliding glass doors with the words FIELD TRAINING etched on them, Bernie had flashbacks to the obstacle courses she'd mastered during basic training when she'd first arrived. She had run around the indoor track inside the gigantic gymnasium more times than she could count. But the moment she stepped inside, she was surprised to find that the familiar exercise equipment had been replaced by what looked like a random pile of haphazard junk.

"What's going on?" she wondered.

"Not sure," answered Jarvis, looking puzzled. "Maybe some kind of recycling program?"

"Better than that!" said a booming voice. Wheeling around, Bernie saw a dashing hamster stride onto the field.

He was big—nearly as tall as Jarvis—barrel chested, and wore a sparkling silver jumpsuit. His mustachelike whiskers were carefully waxed and curled, and his eyes sparkled with intensity.

Jarvis gaped at the heroic-looking hamster. "No way. NO WAY! That's Jerome Sleekwhisker," he squeaked.

"Who?" asked Bernie, puzzled.

"Only the greatest space explorer of all time," Jarvis whispered. Bernie thought her starstruck friend looked like he was about to faint. He gazed at Bernie, his eyes burning with feverish fandom. "You're not reacting. Didn't you hear me? I said, the . . . greatest . . . space explorer . . . of . . . all . . . TIME! Bigger than Neil Armstrong! He's been across the galaxy and back! The humans don't even know half of all that he's done."

"Okay . . ." Bernie began.

"Okay? I tell you that and all you can say is *okay?*" said Jarvis. "Wow. That's like saying Neil deGrasse Tyson is just some science-y dude that happens to like stars a little bit."

"But he is a science-y dude," began Bernie. Fortunately, she was spared a further lecture from Jarvis when Sleekwhisker's booming voice overwhelmed their whispered exchange.

"What you're seeing here is the best space training equipment money can buy," the jovial hamster said, gesturing expansively at the assorted tin soup cans, sprinkler equipment, faded kiddie pool and ancient-looking toys. Jarvis noticed Bernie's disappointed glance and couldn't help defending his hero.

"Okay, well, I know it looks more like the best equipment you could buy for five cents," Jarvis whispered to Bernie. But then he quickly added, "But I'm sure he knows what he's doing. After all he's—"

"The greatest space explorer of all time. Yeah, you said," Bernie whispered back. She leveled a skeptical glance at the shoddy equipment, then at the big hamster.

"Um, did Gadget approve all this?" asked Bernie. When it came to equipment and tech, this looked like exactly the opposite of Mouse Watch standards. To Bernie, it looked a lot more like the stuff she'd grown up with in Thousand Acorns. In the mouse village, everyday human items were cleaned up and modified to suit mouse-size needs.

"Gadget knows all about it," boomed the big hamster. He thrust his paw out for them to shake and announced, "Commander Jerome Sleekwhisker, space explorer extraordinaire. I've been on over thirty missions, twenty-eight of which I designed myself. Homemade rockets are a specialty of mine." He winked and added, "The last two missions were with NASA and SPACE-X. I'm also the first hamster test pilot ever to get an official commendation from the president of the United States."

Jarvis was dumbfounded as he automatically shook

the proffered paw. Bernie couldn't help being a bit impressed, too.

"I trained on equipment just like this, and since Gadget entrusted me with training you to be mousetronauts, she agreed to let me do things my way," he added.

Bernie hardly knew what to think about the bombastic hamster, but there was something about his confidence that was kind of soothing.

"Did you say that you've been up to space thirty times?" asked Bernie nervously.

"Sure did," said Sleekwhisker, preening a bit. "First time, I wasn't much older than you. I always wanted to see the stars and couldn't wait to get up there."

"What was it like?" asked Jarvis eagerly. "I mean, I've seen the documentaries on MouseTube about you," he added. "But, seriously, was it as amazing as you made it sound?"

"It is everything you can imagine and MORE!" said Sleekwhisker. His gaze grew distant, recalling fond memories. "The view of Earth from up there really puts things into perspective." He glanced back at Bernie and Jarvis and grinned. "It's also fun! Antigravity is the best, especially when you're a big guy like me!"

He let out a jolly chortle, and Bernie couldn't help but grin. *Maybe this won't be as bad as I thought. I gotta admit maybe Jarvis is right. Sleekwhisker apparently knows what he's doing and he seems supercool.*

"How soon can we get started?" asked Jarvis, eagerly rubbing his paws together.

"Right now!" said Sleekwhisker. The big hamster strode to a whiteboard that had a surprisingly well-drawn diagram on it with neatly lettered mission objectives. The organized notes stood in sharp contrast to the junky-looking "training equipment" scattered around the spacious facility.

Sleekwhisker ran a paw along his neatly curled whiskers, twirling them before gesturing at the first of three bullet points on the board. "Okay, so before we put you through the gauntlet, let's go over the mission, shall we? This is a simple breakdown of your roles and what we hope to accomplish. Number one . . ."

Sleekwhisker tapped the board next to the first line. "Slinktail, Gadget has a lot of confidence in your drone piloting and tech skills. She's asked that you be in charge of the satellite launch systems on the ship. Your main duties will be to work closely with Tony, our new AI system, and ensure that the satellite detaches properly from the ship and is piloted into position. Also, if anything goes wrong with the programming or there's a bug in the system, it'll be up to that genius noggin of yours to fix it and fast."

Jarvis nodded, grinning. "I can do that."

Bernie thought he looked confident and much more assured than usual. She knew this was because when it came to anything having to do with drones or computers, Jarvis was an expert.

Sleekwhisker flicked at an imaginary piece of dust on his sparkling clean jumpsuit and then, turning to Bernie, the big hamster said, "Skampersky, Gadget says that in spite of your minisize, you have twice as much guts as the biggest mouse on campus." He gestured to a drawing of a mouse attached to a long cable that extended outside of the spaceship capsule. "Once we achieve orbit, you'll be doing a spacewalk to ensure that the satellite is protected. You'll be equipped with a digital lasso that can harness and detonate any and all space debris out of the way so that the satellite can be placed where it can function without danger. It'll take lightning reflexes, which Gadget has assured me that you have."

"She's great," said Jarvis enthusiastically. "She's one of the best at using a digital lasso! We've been practicing it in the VR simulators, right, B?"

Bernie felt his friendly nudge, but she didn't say a word. Her eyes were trained at the horrific drawing depicting her—Bernie Skampersky—floating in outer space with nothing but a skinny tube attaching her to a tin-can ship. She was afraid that if she opened her mouth, all that would come out would be a frightened squeak!

Sleekwhisker nodded his approval. "That's good. And remember Skampersky, in space even the smallest asteroid can do a ton of damage. They're speeding by much faster than you realize. One hit from a decent-size rock and the entire satellite could explode!"

Oh great, thought Bernie miserably.

Sleek continued, "So, we'll be depending on your courage and radical sharpshooting skills to allow Slinktail to pilot that satellite into position. Think you can handle that?"

Sleekwhisker grinned at her. He misinterpreted Bernie's lack of response as being too enthusiastic to speak.

"Know just how you're feeling. I remember when I got to do my first spacewalk. It completely changed my life." Sleekwhisker smiled at the memory, his eyes glazing over in happiness. "I was floating free in a star-studded universe with hardly anything attaching me to the ship but a tiny lifeline. Ahhhh . . . You're so lucky!"

It was the second time someone had told Bernie she was lucky for getting to do something that filled her with terror. She gulped, feeling once again the churn of nausea in her stomach. She managed a tiny nod and a weak smile for the commander. Sleekwhisker didn't seem to notice her discomfort.

"Number two," he continued, turning back to the board. "This part of the mission is pretty simple. Gadget wants us to gather data on the current effects of climate change by observing the land masses on Earth from space. The ship is equipped with a high-powered telescope and the latest and greatest meteorological monitoring equipment. I'll be overseeing that part of the mission."

He tapped the third and final point with a thoughtful expression. "And finally, the last and most top secret part of the mission: the Moonshot."

Bernie noticed that there wasn't anything written next to the word *Moonshot*.

"Oh, I get it," said Jarvis. "Because we rescued the Milk Saucer from the SS *Moon*, it's the code name, right? Moonshot. I like it!"

For Bernie, just seeing the words *moon* and *shot* next to each other gave her the heebie-jeebies. It sounded like a planet exploding.

"Nope," said Sleekwhisker.

"Oh, then . . . I know . . . It's because we'll use the gravitational pull of the moon to slingshot us back to Earth because our fuel will be low. Is that it?" Jarvis asked.

Bernie knew that Jarvis hated not knowing the answer to a secret or a puzzle. But the furry hamster just shook his head and winked. "I won't be unboxing this little secret until we're up there, but just know that you both are in for the surprise of your young lives."

Bernie noticed that in Sleekwhisker's drawing, there

was a big, mysterious question mark hanging in the space between Earth and the moon. She shivered.

"So, all in all, fairly straightforward on the mission objectives. If there are no questions, let's get on to the fun stuff!" Sleekwhisker grinned. Bernie had a ton of questions, most of them about safety and how to avoid dying, but her mouth was so dry from panic she couldn't ask one even if she'd wanted to.

"Now then, the first thing we're going to do is get you used to G forces. We're talking G for *gravity*, not *gerbils*," he added with a chortle. "Gerbil forces would be ridiculous."

"Uhhh . . . right," said Jarvis, looking confused.

Bernie had no idea what to expect as the big hamster led them across the turf to a tin soup can that was fastened on top of a rotating sprinkler head. Glancing inside the can, she recognized two chairs from the Springtime Nancy dollhouse, a line of human dolls and accessories that her mom obsessively collected and repurposed. The chairs were made of pink molded plastic and had been outfitted with makeshift harnesses crafted from pipe cleaners.

"I'd put my equipment up against any current space program's tech any day of the week. All those gadgets, pah!" Sleekwhisker waved his paw dismissively. "Nothing like good old-fashioned stuff to make a hamsternaut or, in your case, a *mousetronaut* strong!"

He paused with his hands on his hips, surveying them both closely. "I've found, in my vast experiences, that the simplest solutions are always the best. So many rodents fail because they don't see the solutions that are right there in front of their faces! Who needs high tech when low tech works just fine? Now, hop inside, you two!"

Bernie and Jarvis did as they were told. Bernie was happy to find that the improvised chairs, although a bit uncomfortable, seemed solidly put together. She lowered the pipe cleaner harness, snapping it into place with two alligator clips.

"When I turn the hose on, the can is going to spin. We're gonna get you up to about 4G, just like the centrifuge they use at NASA. You'll feel flat as a pancake, but don't worry—it'll pass. The idea here is that when the rocket takes off, it'll feel much the same. Ready?"

Bernie hardly had time to say, "Yes," before Sleekwhisker closed the lid of the can. She glanced over at Jarvis and noticed, for the first time, he looked a little uneasy. The young rat experienced a lot of motion sickness when they'd ridden the Secret Watcher International Subway System (S.W.I.S.S.)—the Mouse Watch's high-speed Maglev train.

"Did you bring the motion sickness medicine that Gadget made you?" asked Bernie.

Jarvis shook his head. "I don't know what I was thinking! I forgot it back in my room!"

Seeing him pale and nervous like this actually emboldened Bernie. Having a friend going through some of the anxiety that had been raging inside of her for the past twenty-four hours mustered up a protective instinct inside of her.

"It's gonna be okay, Jarvie. It's like you said, this Sleekwhisker guy seems to know what he's doing. It'll all be over before you know it. Remember, you're gonna get to go to space! It's your dream come true!"

Jarvis was still pale, but he nodded and gritted his teeth, steeling himself for the upcoming ride.

The can started to spin slowly at first. Bernie imagined that Sleekwhisker was probably adjusting the water pressure in the hose a bit at a time to get them used to the sensation of spinning on the sprinkler head. Bernie had watched a lot of MouseTube videos of humans at amusement parks. She'd secretly envied them and had often wished she could have experienced some of the fun. Looking at what they were doing through that lens made riding in the can more exciting.

It's just a carnival ride like the Tilt-A-Whirl, that's all, Bernie told herself.

The spinning increased. Bernie felt the can shake as it turned faster and faster on the spinning sprinkler head. She was going really fast now, in tight concentric circles, whirling in a way that made everything around her look blurry.

A big grin spread across Bernie's face. This was actually fun! She let out a loud "WHOOP!" and raised her paws in the air just like she'd seen kids do on the Tilt-A-Whirl in the human carnivals.

The ride was just as Sleekwhisker described. There was a moment or two when Bernie really did feel like she'd been squashed flat as a pancake. But before she knew it, the can was slowing to a stop. Sleekwhisker opened the lid and Bernie jumped out, chattering excitedly.

"Thatwassocool!Canwegoagain?" The words came out in a rush.

Sleekwhisker laughed and slapped her on the back. "I felt the same way at your age!" he boomed. "You're gonna do great! You're just like me!"

For the moment, the thrill of the ride made her feel like her old self again. Any thoughts of aliens were far from her mind. In fact, just having Sleekwhisker around made her feel like maybe she was being silly. After all, he would have said something if he'd ever seen one during his missions.

I actually think I can do this, she told herself. *I just need to relax about it.*

The thought made her feel better. Jarvis emerged much more slowly, gripping the sides of the can for support and looking a bit green in the cheeks. But, to Bernie's surprise, he managed not to throw up. Instead, he gave them a quivering thumbs-up.

"Way to go, Jarvie!" said Bernie.

"Well done!" roared Sleekwhisker. "Want to go again?"

Jarvis stared at him with wide eyes. "D-do we have to, Commander?" he stuttered.

"HAW! Not yet," said Sleekwhisker. "And don't bother with that Commander nonsense. Call me Sleek, all my friends do."

"O-okay, Sleek," said Jarvis, clearly a little starstruck.

The hamster rubbed his paws together. "Now then, we've got all kinds of other fun training to do. The launch is only three days away and we've got to get cracking!"

Berne and Jarvis stared at him with stunned expressions. *Three days?* thought Bernie. *I had no idea it was happening so fast!*

Feeling much better than she had just a few hours ago, Bernie trotted after the big hamster as he led her over to more of his improvised training equipment. *I'm going to beat this!* she thought. *I'm going to go into outer space and I'm going to come back a hero!* The more encouraging words she told herself, the bolder she felt. And as she joined Sleek at the edge of the kiddie pool, she whispered to herself, "Never underestimate Bernie Skampersky. I'm small, but I'm MIGHTY!"

CHAPTER 6

"Tony, activate underwater breathing," said Bernie.

Initiated, replied Tony.

She heard tiny servos turn inside of hidden compartments next to her goggle lenses. Seconds later, a microthin breathing apparatus emerged and covered Bernie's nose and mouth. The goggles themselves were, of course, not only waterproof but also enhanced to provide detailed descriptions of everything she saw while submerged.

Are you getting enough air? asked Tony, sounding concerned. "I can totally adjust it to whatever's comfortable."

"Feels great," said Bernie. "Thanks."

No prob, said the AI.

Bernie had gotten so comfortable with Tony that, in spite of knowing better, she actually was thinking of him as a real person. His casual slang was so convincing that it was hard to picture a computer server somewhere running a program.

As she moved her goggles from her forehead over her eyes, she couldn't help wondering if Tony sounded the same way to Jarvis. Did he speak to her friend the same way he spoke to her?

Bernie dove into the kiddie pool and, as instructed, began to navigate the series of rings and weighted objects that Sleekwhisker had put there. Going through the obstacle course was an exercise meant to simulate the lack of gravity in space. A mousetronaut had to learn how to float around the cabin of a spacecraft without bumping into anything delicate.

Jarvis had learned to swim on their last mission but still wasn't very good at it. His fear of water made doing the test a bit more challenging than it would have been otherwise, but Bernie saw by his expression that he was determined to succeed.

As they swam, Bernie gave him a thumbs-up. Jarvis, looking pale but focused behind his glowing goggles, returned the gesture and awkwardly half swam, half dogpaddled his way through a row of notebook binder rings, somehow managing not to bang into a single one of the edges.

Bernie was reminded that everyday objects that humans used were still useful if resourceful mice noticed them in new ways. She'd gotten so comfortable with Gadget's mouse-size inventions and furniture that it had been easy to forget how the other rodents in the world had to rely on improvising and repurposing human items to fit their needs. She'd grown up with spools of thread for coffee tables and matchboxes as dresser drawers. It made her appreciate her parents' ingenuity. Suddenly, she felt a pang in her chest over how much she missed them.

When I call Mom and Dad tonight, I'll tell them all about the mission, thought Bernie. She was good about calling them every day, but now that she knew the launch was happening so soon, she wanted to make sure she had plenty of time to tell them good-bye.

Hopefully not permanently, she thought as she swam.

As Bernie glided through the last ring and tapped the bottle cap that Sleekwhisker had positioned there as a finish line, her stomach did a little flip-flop. Just thinking about the rocket launch still made her nervous, but she was doing a whole lot better now that Sleek was overseeing her training.

He's the bravest mouse I've ever met! thought Bernie. *I'm starting to get why Jarvis admires him so much. Just having him in charge makes me feel safe. If he thinks I'm a lot like him, then . . . seriously . . . what do I have to worry about?*

When she crawled up the plastic ramp and out of the

water at the end of the obstacle course, Sleek pushed down the button on a human-size digital stopwatch.

"One minute forty-five," he announced. "Good job, Skampersky. Impressive!" He glanced at Jarvis and added, "And not too bad for you, Slinktail. There's room for improvement, but not too bad."

Jarvis smiled gratefully. Bernie watched him activate his goggles' fur-drying mechanism, the device sending out tiny drones with spinning fans that raced up and down his jumpsuit and evaporated every drop of water. She had to admire her friend's courage.

He's really improved a lot since he got here, she mused. *The fraidy-rat I used to know is practically gone!*

After activating her own dryer drones, Bernie took her place next to Jarvis, awaiting further instruction from their cool new instructor.

"We'll hit the boot tomorrow," said Sleek. "You'll be laced up inside and tossed into a rotating dryer." He raised his paw before Jarvis could object. "Don't worry, the heating mechanism has been taken out. It's perfectly safe. But get ready for the bumpiest ride of your life. It's the best simulation for an asteroid field I've ever come up with."

Bernie grinned. In his own way, Sleek was an inventor just like Gadget, except that he used everyday objects in ingenious ways. She felt her admiration growing for the hamstronaut more and more.

"But before you call it quits for the day, I'd like you to get some target practice in, Skampersky. Hit the laser-tag court for an hour or two. Those meteorites we'll be encountering up there aren't going to destroy themselves."

"Excuse me, sir, I mean . . . Sleek," said Bernie.

"Hmm?" asked Sleekwhisker.

"I was just wondering if . . . well . . ." Bernie suddenly felt herself growing shy and tongue-tied. "Will you be talking to us over the radio while we're up in space?" she asked. She wanted to add that it would make her feel so much better to have his calm, reassuring presence there in her ear, but she couldn't quite manage it.

"I'm afraid that's not an option . . ." began the commander.

Bernie's heart sank. But then Sleek broke into a huge smile and said, "Because I'm going with you!"

"You are?" exclaimed Bernie and Jarvis at the same time. Sleekwhisker patted them both on the back and nodded. "Of course I am. Been the plan all along! What, did you think that Tony was going to steer the ship? No offense, but I'm a thousand times better at it than any AI."

Tony's voice in Bernie's goggles let out a loud, skeptical *Hrmph!* at that statement.

If Bernie had known Sleekwhisker better, she would have thrown her arms around the hamster in a big hug. It was a total relief to think of him up there in space with them! Being the professional Level Two agent that she was, though, she simply beamed back at him and offered a sharp salute. Sleek chuckled, sending his chubby hamster cheeks quivering as he returned the gesture.

"After target practice, get some good rest tonight. Tomorrow's the last day of training and then, BOOM! We're off to space!"

"Woo-hoo!" exclaimed Jarvis in an unusually loud burst of enthusiasm.

They followed the commander out of the training room. As they merged into the busy Mouse Watch hallways, Bernie noticed the admiring looks, sighs, and whispers from many of the female agents as the famous hamster walked by.

Jarvis, noticing too, puffed out his chest a little as he walked and tried to glom on to the attention. A couple of cute young agents about Bernie's age smiled at Jarvis and he grinned back, blushing furiously.

Bernie shot them both an icy look.

"Hey, Jarvie. After I finish target practice, how about a game of Mice and Dice?" she suggested, grabbing the sleeve of his hoodie and diverting his attention away from the giggling mice.

"Huh? Oh, yeah, sure!" said Jarvis, coming back to himself.

Bernie shot the giggling females an eye roll. She gently pushed Jarvis in the direction of his dormitory, then rushed off to the VR simulator.

After scanning her handprint at the door, Bernie entered the familiar chamber. When she'd first arrived, she and Jarvis had been put through some Level One rescue training in this room. As she buckled into one of the high-tech chairs and donned her haptic gloves and VR helmet, she flashed back on those early days. Everything at that time had been so new and exciting!

Hard to believe I could have ever thought that Jarvie was a double agent, Bernie mused. The thought was totally ridiculous now that she knew him.

A screen materialized in her headset, offering a wide array of apps. Her gloved hands moved through the air, scrolling through several menus until she found *Target Practice.*

When she made the selection, a light tone chimed in her ear. Bernie felt the chair slowly lift into the air. It was designed so that she stayed strapped in while her arms and legs could move freely. The simulations that Gadget had programmed were beyond impressive. The worlds that Bernie could visit in VR were so convincing and tactile, it was always a bit disorienting when she finished one of the programs. Usually, the laser tag sim was in a dark maze with a pulse-pounding hip-hop soundtrack. But, perhaps at Sleekwhisker's request, Bernie noticed that Gadget had programmed a new modification.

Asteroid Challenge.

Bernie selected the mod. A star-studded vista filled her vision, and suddenly, quite realistically, Bernie felt like she was floating in outer space! Even though some part of her knew that it was VR, she felt a surge of terror as the inky blackness stretched endlessly around her.

Calm down!

It took some effort, but Bernie forced herself to breathe normally. Reaching down to her side, her haptic glove felt the handle of the digital lasso.

Here goes.

At the touch of her paw on the handle, a torrent of meteorites came hurtling toward her. A thrumming, heavy dub step soundtrack filled her ears. Without thinking, her training kicked into gear and Bernie took aim.

BOOM! BOOM! BOOM!

Bernie lassoed each meteorite with her glowing digital rope and whipped them aside to detonate out of harm's way. Exploding space rocks flew right and left. Bernie was an expert at *Digital Lasso*. On the scoreboard, she consistently ranked in the top twenty. Her screen name, "BernItUp," was at the top of the boards and she was well-known among the other players as someone not to trifle with!

As she lost herself in the game, Bernie felt a renewed

optimism about the mission. It was a good reminder that as a Level Two agent she'd become a lot more skilled than she often gave herself credit for.

By the time the simulation ended, Bernie was feeling much better about the entire mission. She decided that she should probably head back to her dorm and give her parents a call.

The corridors were bustling with the postdinner crowd. At this time of the evening, many agents liked to hang out in the cafeteria for dessert and hazelnut tea. There was usually an assortment of dried fruit and sweet cheeses (including her favorite, apricot Stilton).

As Bernie made her way through the crowd of furry agents, she picked up a disturbing snatch of conversation between two high-ranking agents.

". . . and she's basically still a kid!" said a lanky female agent with large front teeth. "I could never have gone on a space mission at Skampersky's age. I'd have been scared out of my mind!"

"Tell me about it," said a burly older mouse with gray whiskers. "If you ask me, Gadget is taking a huge risk. Not only that, but I think this Sleektail guy is way too big for his britches . . . literally. He's the hugest mouse I've ever seen!"

"He's a hamster, Dennis," said the lanky female.

"Whatever," groused Dennis, waving away the

distinction. "He's just a MouseTube celebrity who's only in it for the fame and glory. That's not what the Watch stands for." His eyes narrowed with suspicion. "Hey, I just thought of something. Do hamsters even have tails?"

"Yes, little ones," said the lanky mouse.

"Well, it doesn't seem like a suitable name. I mean, why's he even called Sleektail? Sleek*bottom* would be better."

The lanky mouse ran a tired paw over her eyes and said, "If Gadget says he's okay, then he's okay by me. I'm a lot more worried about the kid than the hamster."

"These kids and their MouseTube. When I was a mouseling the only tube I needed was left over from a paper towel roll and I loved it," he grumbled.

Bernie was much shorter than ninety-nine percent of the other agents, which made it pretty easy to eavesdrop without being noticed. The two agents didn't even see her standing beside them.

With the lanky agent's words, *I'd have been scared out of my mind*, ringing in her ears, Bernie slowly walked down the gleaming hallway to the dormitories. She entered her room and shakily closed the door behind her. Her heart thudded, and her old anxieties, which had been eased somewhat by her time spent running simulations with Sleek, were threatening to return.

"Get it together," Bernie whispered to herself. "Remember your training. You've got this. Sleek said so."

It was amazing how fast her confidence could disappear. One minute she'd been feeling like everything might work out okay, but then, at the slightest comment from her peers, her good feelings had vanished. There was something about the way they'd talked about her and Sleek that made her feel extrajumbly inside.

If the rest of the agents aren't feeling confident about me going on the mission, why should I? Bernie wondered. She usually had complete and total confidence in everything Gadget said or did. But maybe it was because she was confronting a childhood fear or maybe something else, but for some reason the older agents' lack of confidence hit her hard.

Bernie took a long, steadying breath. She smoothed her tower of blue hair into place, sat on the edge of her bunk, and picked up her phone.

After a couple of rings, the warm voice of her father answered. "Bernie-pie!" he exclaimed. Bernie felt a warm glow inside when she heard her dad's favorite nickname for her.

"Hi, Dad. I really miss you guys!"

"We miss you, too! How's everything in secret agent land?"

Bernie hesitated. For a brief moment she thought about blurting out all her fears and anxieties but then decided not to. She didn't want her father to worry even more than he already did. It was hard enough, she knew, having a daughter who was a Mouse Watch agent. She'd fought so hard to get them to agree to let her join in the first place.

"It's great, Dad. I'm going to space!"

"What?" said Bernie's dad. "You're kidding!" She heard her dad's voice fade a little as he moved away from the phone. "Hey, Susie, Bernie's going to space!"

"She's got her own place? Why isn't she living in the dorms?" came Bernie's mom's faint reply.

"Space!" shouted her dad. "Space!"

"If you need space, just say so," said Bernie's mom. "Why don't you go work in the garage?"

Bernie interrupted, "Dad, I gotta go, but I just wanted to tell you guys that I love you."

"We love you, too, Bernie-pie," said her dad.

As Bernie hung up the phone, she heard her dad trying to explain to her mom what was going on, and she chuckled, shaking her head.

After grabbing some cheese and crackers from the snack machine, Bernie went to the little common room where she usually met her friends. Jarvis and Juno were already there, settling in for a long, fun night of adventure. Bernie sighed contentedly as she joined them. Playing Mice and Dice was exactly what she needed to take her mind off the launch. As game master, Jarvis was always good about slipping brain teasers and puzzles into each campaign, and she could really use some mental distraction.

As they snacked and set up the game board, the conversation turned to Sleekwhisker.

"It sure makes me feel more confident knowing that Sleek's going with us," said Bernie, hoping to make herself feel better by saying positive thoughts out loud. She placed her mouse elf figurine on the gaming grid. "He's so awesome."

"Yeah, can you imagine the stuff he's seen?" asked Jarvis. He peeked his head up from behind his game master's screen and grinned. "We're talkin' asteroids, planets, maybe even alien life! Oops, sorry," he added, noticing Bernie's face go pale.

"Wait, what?" said Juno, with a nervous glance at Bernie. "Who said anything about aliens? There's no such thing as aliens."

"No, you're right. I was just kidding, there's no aliens. Total hoax," said Jarvis.

Bernie didn't like to be reminded about her secret fear.

"Hey, while you're up there, take a picture of Earth for me, will you?" said Juno. "That would be cool to see." Her expression turned wistful. "I know it's only supposed to last four days, but I bet it's gonna feel like a lifetime. I really want you guys to get back here safe and sound as soon as possible."

"Oh, don't worry, Juno," said Jarvis. "Gadget's tech never fails. Tony will be in control of everything up there, and we have Commander Sleek, too. I'd hate to think of you being nervous the whole time we're up there."

"Nervous? Who said anything about being nervous?" Juno said. "I just don't want to put our campaign on hold too long when we're about to face the three-headed zombie king."

And as she reached for another slice of cheese to put on a cracker, Bernie realized that Juno had complete and total faith that she and Jarvis were not only coming back safely but that they were also completely qualified to be mousetronauts.

I hope she's right, thought Bernie. *Otherwise, it's going to be pretty hard for her to play Mice and Dice all by herself.*

CHAPTER 7

In spite of trying to reassure herself that everything was going to be fine for the launch, Bernie had another night of terrible sleep. Squishy alien tentacles and strange, otherworldly slime creatures chased her though the night, invading all her dreams.

At first, it was a relief to wake up. But then she remembered what day it was. The reality of what she was about to do came crashing down, and Bernie had to fight off a prickly panic that crawled up her spine, threatening to completely overwhelm her.

"I'm sick," she said, staring at her reflection in the mirror. "I'll tell them I have a fever and I can't go."

Bernie tried to think of ways she could make her forehead feel hot so that she could fool Gadget and Sleek. She briefly considered soaking a washcloth in hot water and holding it on her forehead but knew right away that it was a dumb idea and wouldn't fool anybody.

She noticed something lumpy on her desk chair.

With shaking paws, she reached for the silver-wrapped package. At some point during the night someone with official authority to enter her room must have delivered it.

As she unwrapped the package, she muttered nervously to herself. "I can't do this. I'm gonna tell Sleek that I'm backing out. He'll just have to understand that . . . that it's not for me. I'm just Bernie. I didn't sign up for this."

But when she saw what was in the package, her eyes widened and her whiskers gave a surprised twitch. It was a gleaming silver jumpsuit that had the Mouse Watch logo displayed proudly on the sparkling pocket. Next to it was her name: B. SKAMPERSKY, MOUSETRONAUT. It was just like Sleekwhisker's and had clearly been especially designed for the occasion.

"Mousetronaut. Never thought I'd see my name next to a job description like that," she murmured. Seeing the suit made her feel such an unexpected surge of pride that she knew there was no way she could back out now.

Bernie donned the elegant uniform, controlling her shaking paws as she smoothed it over her tummy. Then, going to the mirror, she carefully finished styling her signature haircut.

"Here we go," she said. "This is it."

She took a deep, steadying breath and walked rather shakily out of her quarters to meet Jarvis and Sleek.

It wasn't hard to find them. They'd arranged to meet at the S.W.I.S.S. station, a hidden location behind an innocent-looking water fountain in the middle of Mouse Watch HQ. The station entrance was supposed to be a secret, but apparently, as always happens, word had gotten out and all the Watchers knew about it. A big throng of well-wishers had crowded the corridor that led to the hidden entrance, and Bernie had to squeeze and shove her way through a tight mass of mouse bodies to get to her companions.

"What kept you?" asked Jarvis. But one look at Bernie's anxious expression and he decided not to pursue the line of questioning any further.

Glancing over, Bernie noticed that Sleek was in his usual rare form, cracking jokes, signing autographs, and winking at his adoring fans.

How can he be so cool under pressure? Bernie wondered. *Am I the only one freaked out about this mission?*

"There's something about that guy I don't like," said Juno, noticing where Bernie was looking. The young rat had squeezed in and was huddled shoulder to shoulder with them.

Jarvis gestured at a swooning trio of Mouse Watch agents who were hanging on Sleekwhisker's every word.

"Seems like you're the only one."

"It's his uniform. Look how perfectly pressed it is. Not a single wrinkle!" Juno added disgustedly. "The guy doesn't have a whisker out of place. He seems obsessive."

Bernie noticed that the hamster's uniform did look especially crisp, his mustache neatly combed. "Probably his training at NASA?" she asked.

"I don't know," Juno said. Her eyes narrowed. "Something's off."

Jarvis looked at his smartwatch. "Hey, we've got to get to the docking bay!" He moved over and tapped Sleekwhisker on the shoulder. "Excuse me, sir. It's T minus fifteen minutes to launch."

"Whoops! Time flies when you're having fun!" boomed Sleek.

The burly hamster gave a final farewell wave, blew some kisses, and after Bernie and Jarvis received a quick good-bye hug and a "good luck" from Juno, Bernie found herself hustling down the old stairway behind the drinking fountain to the S.W.I.S.S.

Bernie emerged from the old, brick passageway into the cathedral-like platform for the Maglev train. Normally, she would have been leading the way, lowering her goggles and calling out, "Hey, S.W.I.S.S.!" to summon the train. But this time, she was content to hang back and let Commander Sleek run the show. She was busy trying to keep her knees and paws from trembling and paced back and forth in order to get her body to calm down.

"Hey, B, don't worry. This entire mission will be over before you know it," whispered Jarvis encouragingly. "Would you like to hear a riddle?"

Bernie remembered how she'd helped Jarvis when he was panicking on the sub by giving him puzzles to solve.

"Sure, why not," mumbled Bernie. One of the things that they both shared was a love for puzzles of all kinds.

As the gleaming white S.W.I.S.S. train pulled up to the platform, Jarvis said, "Here's a fun one. *At night they come without being gathered and by day they depart without being scattered.*"

Bernie turned the puzzle over in her mind as she buckled herself into her train seat. It was so strange to suddenly have the shoe on the other foot, to be the one calmed down by her friend instead of the other way around. Bernie found it difficult to concentrate on the riddle as the train lurched into gear and sped away down the hidden magnetic tracks. She was too distracted by the thought of the rocket launch.

"Next stop, Mission Control!" announced Sleek.

Bernie gulped. *This is actually happening!* Jarvis noticed how pale she was. He removed a small packet from his jumpsuit pocket and offered her a red tablet.

"Need one of Gadget's motion sickness cures? These ones taste like raspberry with a hint of lime." Bernie shook her head. "No? Are you sure? You look a little pale."

Bernie smiled weakly. Jarvis patted her arm and returned the packet to his suit.

The trip to Mission Control was, like all destinations on the high-speed train, over practically before it started. When the S.W.I.S.S. whooshed to a stop, Bernie unbuckled her harness and disembarked onto an outdoor destination platform.

She gazed around. It certainly wasn't what Bernie had expected. Up until then, she'd thought the S.W.I.S.S. only traveled underground. The station platforms were usually hidden in places dark and dank—converted sewers that had been abandoned or neglected areas of subway tunnels.

But this time, Bernie was surprised to see that this S.W.I.S.S. station was aboveground and commanded a sweeping, majestic view of the outdoors.

To her left was a gigantic, modern white building that was shaped kind of like an eyebrow on a hill. The building had apparently once been a human civic arts center, for it had a dilapidated sign with missing letters on it indicating that it had been abandoned and moved to a new location. A small, mouse-size sign that read, MISSION CONTROL had been posted on a little mound next to it. Bernie recognized Sleek's distinctive, immaculate handwriting right away, and it was a reminder of just how relatively new the Mouse Watch space program really was.

But in a steep valley just below her was the sight she'd been dreading, the one that gave her the shivers as soon as she looked at it. There, poised regally on a concrete launchpad, was the rocket that she would soon be boarding.

I can't believe I'm going up in that thing!

The torpedo-shaped ship wasn't nearly as big as a human-size rocket. Bernie had seen plenty of those on MouseTube. This one was about the size of a very large hobby-store model. Bernie knew that most of the toy versions that humans used were constructed out of a cardboard tube with a plastic nose cone and cheap parachute inside of them. Thankfully, at first glance, Gadget's design appeared to be made of much stronger stuff. It didn't bring Bernie a whole lot of comfort, but it at least helped to know that it was built better than Sleekwhisker's training equipment.

I can hear that your breathing has accelerated, said Tony. *Since I've been listening to the anxieties you've been sharing with your friends about space, I'm assuming that's the reason.*

Bernie felt a flicker of annoyance at the AI. She'd forgotten that it was always around and listening in on conversations.

"Well, yeah," said Bernie sharply. "I'm a bit upset, okay?"

I might be able to help, said Tony. *I can tell you facts about the rocket that you're about to board. It's made of all the latest Mouse Watch tech and has a navigation system that's superior to even the top human space programs. I'll be controlling everything, so you have nothing to worry about. In spite of what Commander Sleek says, I am a better pilot than he is.*

Bernie wondered briefly why Commander Sleek had told her that he was going to be doing Tony's job, but then put it out of her head. *He's just used to doing things old style,* she thought. *Probably not used to such high-tech stuff. After all, he had us train in a tin can strapped to a sprinkler head.*

She chuckled to herself. Thinking of the burly hamster gave her a little comfort. But just a little. Alarm bells were still going off inside her brain.

"Thanks, Tony," she murmured.

Anytime, the AI replied. *I'm always here if you need me.*

Bernie looked more closely at the rocket launch area and noticed that the concrete platform around the launch-pad was surrounded by the remains of a human playground. Bernie was surprised to see a rusty slide and a towering metal swing set in the middle of what should have been a

wide, open field. Seeing those big human playthings nearby made the scale of the rocket appear very small. From where Bernie stood, it seemed that the top of the rocket's capsule was barely tall enough to stand side by side with the bottom of the nearest hanging swing.

How could a tiny mouse like me be blasted into something so vast and incomprehensibly huge as outer space? she thought. *I really shouldn't be doing this. I should be back at HQ in my nice soft bed.*

Commander Sleekwhisker noticed Bernie staring with a look of horror at the rocket.

"Yeah, I wish that stuff wasn't there either. I was told by Gadget that there used to be a park here," he said, misinterpreting the object of her gaze. "The swings and slide were much too big for the Mouse Watch excavation equipment to move, so they just left them where they stood. But on the bright side, it does kind of make a for a pretty picture, don't you think? Reminds us about all the human children we've helped save over the years."

Bernie hadn't thought of it at all that way.

Her gaze was torn from the launchpad as she felt Jarvis gently steer her shoulders toward the Mission Control building nearby. As the three of them walked through a set of automatic glass doors and entered the facility, Bernie tried desperately to control her rapid breathing, telling herself over and over again to calm down.

Relax! Tony's got this under control. Gadget knows what she's doing. . . .

But as hard as she tried, for some reason her body wouldn't obey what her mind was telling her. Thankfully, she was distracted when Jarvis asked, "Hey! Did you figure out the answer to my riddle?"

"No, what is it?" mumbled Bernie.

"You don't want to figure it out? How about a guess?" encouraged Jarvis. *"At night they come without being gathered and by day they depart without being scattered."*

When Bernie didn't try to answer, he smiled and announced, "Stars! The answer's *stars.* I thought you'd get that one in two seconds!"

Bernie shrugged. She knew that she was being completely unlike her normal self, but until the mission was over and her paws were safely back down on Earth, she didn't know if she could even manage a smile. She knew she'd feel a WHOLE lot better after her space walk was over and she'd done her job to ensure that the satellite was in position. Now that it was becoming real, the thought of floating out there in space filled her stomach with flip-flopping butterflies.

Bernie couldn't have cared less about puzzles at that moment. Her eyes now were riveted on all the space photographs that lined the walls of the building. Giant panoramas of the moon, Mars, and Venus were prominently displayed on every square inch of wall space. Standing beneath the photos, important-looking mice were drinking coffee next to a small coffee cart. Bernie noticed that many of them wore white lab coats, and as they passed by, she overheard them conversing quietly about trajectories, astrophysics, and mathematics.

Jarvis glanced at his smartwatch. "Ooo! We'll be boarding in just a few minutes. Don't worry, I'll be right beside you the whole time."

Those next few minutes felt like years to Bernie. She numbly went through the motions as Mouse Watch technicians helped her into her mousetronaut suit and helmet. Then, as if sleepwalking in a dream, she was led out to the platform for the USS *Mozzarella*.

"Good luck, Skampersky!" said a cheery voice. Bernie glanced over at a pretty mouse with spiky black hair who stood nearby, holding a clipboard. "You go, girl!" she said.

"Thanks," Bernie replied. She managed a weak grin back and offered a feeble thumbs-up.

The autumn morning air was crisp, and the bright California sunlight cast dappled shadows on the rocket through the twisted branches of the nearby oaks, which had been pruned back around the rocket to allow for a safe ascent.

The three mousetronauts couldn't feel the cool air through their helmets, but Bernie wished at that moment that she'd been allowed at least one last, good sniff of Earth's atmosphere before boarding the rocket.

The accordion-style doors slid shut and the elevator slowly rose up the tall gantry tower. Through the glass of her helmet, Bernie saw the ground receding below, the words HAPPY TRAVELS stenciled on the roof of the Mission Control building. She realized that the letters could only be seen from above by the mousetronauts who were about to embark on their space journey, but rather than making her feel excited, it made her feel a wave of homesickness.

I haven't even left yet and I can't wait to get back, she thought.

Jarvis chatted excitedly with Commander Sleekwhisker through the radio in his suit as they boarded the rocket and found their seats.

"This totally reminds me of episode one of *MouseTrek*," he said happily. "That's when they first decided to go into space using Worm Drive. Hey, Sleek, how fast does this ship go? Can we go into hyperspace? What about plasma thrusters, we've got those, right?"

As Bernie buckled herself into her chair, she heard Sleek chuckle and reply, "You've been watching way too much television, Slinktail."

Jarvis couldn't stop chattering as he looked around

at the futuristic controls and the many various blinking touch-screen panels and monitors on board the ship. Bernie settled into her padded chair and pulled her seat belt across her chest, triple-checking that the buckle was securely fastened.

The three chairs in the cockpit were tilted back so that each one looked up at the ceiling. Bernie knew that once they were in space, it wouldn't matter what direction she was facing because the capsule would be free floating. Glancing to the side, she noticed that the inside of the capsule was actually a lot bigger than she'd thought it would be. There was a salon with a dinette table and bench seats. She could see cleverly constructed cabinets everywhere and knew that most of them were filled with dehydrated food and supplies. Most of the area to her right was devoted to the various touch screens and displays, but she also saw a series of cabins that she knew housed their sleeping bunks.

"What will it be like to sleep in space?" she wondered aloud. "Will I just be floating around? How will I stay under the covers?"

Tony was quick to answer. The familiar, chipper AI voice said, *In space, you can sleep in any position. Here on the* Mozz *(that's short for USS Mozzarella), your bunks come with blankets and pillows that have magnetic edges that will stick wherever you want them to.*

"Oh," said Bernie, surprised. "I forgot you were there, Tony. Thanks."

Not a problem, said Tony. *Just let me know if you have any more questions. The hatch is being secured, and we'll be lifting off in one minute and twenty seconds. Now, if you could just flip that red switch marked "Initiate Uplink," I can start communicating with the shipboard computer.*

Hearing the time left to countdown sent a jolt of adrenaline through Bernie's system. *Too late now. You're going up whether you like it or not. You're sealed in and there's no getting out.*

I see your heart rate is increasing again, said Tony. *I can help with that. Would you like to enter another simulated memory? I can multitask while I uplink. How about a virtual taste of some more of that peppermint ice cream you liked so much?*

"Not hungry," said Bernie hoarsely.

I can make other things, suggested Tony.

"Tony. Just . . . please stop. I need to focus."

You got it, boss, said Tony cheerily.

On the one hand, having a virtual escape from the nightmarish reality she was facing actually sounded pretty good to Bernie. However, in spite of her raging anxiety, she felt it was more important to stay on point and focus on the mission at hand.

The blastoff will be over soon, she reminded herself. She wasn't sure which terrified her more, the thought of exploding on the launchpad or being alone drifting in space.

Bernie felt Jarvis's gloved paw reach over and take hers. She gripped his paw tightly, but Jarvis, like a true friend, didn't complain. A monitor above their heads flicked on and she could see various views of Mission Control. Mice in lab coats sat at computers, reviewing preflight checklists. A second screen showed the ground below the rocket.

The last screen was the largest and showed a high definition picture of the endless sapphire-blue sky that was waiting for them above.

T-minus twenty seconds, crackled a voice over Bernie's helmet. *Initiate last checks.*

Bernie listened to the call and responses between the various stations at Mission Control. She thought back to her mission training, rehearsing the underwater swim in her mind so that she'd feel better prepared mentally for floating in space and doing her part of the mission.

Finally, the lead engineer's voice started the ten second countdown.

Ten . . .

Go.

Nine . . .

Go.

Eight . . .

Go.

Seven . . .

Go.

Six . . .

Go.

Five . . .

Go.

Four . . .

Bernie held her breath.

Go.

Three . . .

Go.

Two . . .

Go.

ONE!

BOOOOOM! With one hand gripping Jarvis's paw like a vise and the other clamped down on her seat arm, Bernie's entire body vibrated with the rumbling beneath her seat. On the monitor, she could see a column of fire from the massive rocket engines blast down. Then, a second later, she felt the ship begin to rise.

Lift off, we have lift off! crackled the voice in her helmet. Cheers erupted from the mice inside Mission Control.

Bernie watched with wide, frightened eyes as the blue sky on the monitor grew darker. It gradually gave way to a steady, all-encompassing blackness. Soon, tiny pinpricks of light appeared.

Please don't go BOOM! Please don't go BOOM! thought Bernie.

But then, as the engine roar cut off, and Bernie realized that the rocket hadn't exploded on the launchpad like she'd worried about for so long, she felt a shaky sense of relief. Her breathing, which had been rapid and shallow, slowed as the majesty of space filled the view screen above. Then, her body became light, ascending upward like a helium balloon as it gently pressed against her seat belt harness. Bernie cautiously released her grip from Jarvis's hand.

She'd made it past the first—and scariest—part. Now, all she had left was to face the horribly scary second part— to complete the space walk and hopefully not run into any menacing aliens.

"Soon we'll be back home playing Mice and Dice again," she whispered to herself.

Just hearing the words out loud seemed to help a tiny bit.

And now that they were actually in space, she found, to her surprise, that her anxiety was fading. She glanced around at the efficiently running computer systems. No alarms were blaring. No brightly lit screens were flashing with bright red warning signs.

I . . . I actually think we're gonna be okay.

Impossible as it might have seemed to Bernie just a

little while ago, she found that her fear was slowly being replaced with excitement. She couldn't wait to unbuckle her harness. She wanted to fly around the cabin!

I did it! Bernie thought excitedly. *I'm actually in space!* She was surprised that she was feeling . . . happy. It was a completely unexpected reaction, but welcome. She glanced over to see how Jarvis was doing. The young rat was already out of his harness and floating upward with a big, silly grin on his face.

"This is amazing!" Jarvis called out. "Come on, Bernie!"

Bernie unhooked the latch on her belt and, after an encouraging nod from a smiling Sleek, she felt her body float free.

CHAPTER 8

B ernie had to admit that space was kind of cool. Maybe it was because the launch part had gone off without a hitch, or maybe it was because it turned out Bernie had more courage than even she'd thought possible. Either way, it was nice after three days of anxiety to finally feel like she could have a little fun.

Maybe the real benefit of finding the courage to face your fear is the way it makes you feel about yourself afterward, Bernie wondered. Instead of shame and guilt over giving up, she felt bigger and more confident. She really liked the mouse she was becoming!

"Hey, check me out!" shouted Jarvis. Bernie looked over and saw her friend grinning widely as he swam through the air. "Try it, it's awesome!"

Bernie felt a little unsteady as she floated up. It was

strange, almost like being underwater but without the resistance. She laughed a little wildly as she moved her legs and arms through the air because the sensation was just so . . . new.

"See if you can swim over to me," said Jarvis encouragingly.

Bernie tried, but her arms and legs just flailed in place. She felt like a wild, flopping frog tied to the bottom of a helium balloon! Sleek, who had unbuckled his harness and was floating over to a set of controls on the port side of the capsule, noticed her dilemma.

"To get to where you're going, Skampersky, you have to push off something," he said with a chuckle.

Bernie stopped struggling. Then, stretching her foot downward, she gently pushed off the armrest of her chair with her toes. But without resistance, even that small motion proved to be too much. She immediately zipped upward and conked her helmet on the ceiling.

"Agh!" she shouted.

"Oops! Ha-ha! Good thing you had your helmet on," chuckled Jarvis. "Although, technically you don't need it. The whole ship is filled with oxygen! Just control your motion a little bit; you don't need to use a lot of force." Bernie watched as he turned a somersault. Maybe he was a disaster underwater, but Jarvis was a complete natural in space!

"How can you do that?" Bernie asked, impressed.

Jarvis grinned and shrugged. "I've watched a ton of NASA programs." He pushed off the side of a padded gray wall and floated over to Bernie. She felt him undo the compression clasps at the back of her helmet. Once that was off, she removed her heavy exterior suit and sighed happily. It was a relief to have mobility again. The silver jumpsuit was ideal for moving around inside the capsule, and she found it much easier to gauge the right amount of pressure for floating around the cabin.

Within moments, Jarvis and Bernie were whooping and hollering as they played a quick game of tag, taking turns spinning and tumbling in midair to avoid each other's touch. Captain Sleek allowed them a couple of minutes of fun before waving for them to stop.

"Okay, okay, that's enough. I don't want you two bumping into any navigation equipment and sending us blasting toward Saturn or something."

"Could that really happen?" asked Bernie nervously.

Bernie and Jarvis obeyed immediately. For a moment, she'd forgotten just how dangerous too much horsing around might be.

"Let's not find out," said Sleek gruffly.

Bernie decided that the commander had a good point and vowed to be more careful. It would take many hours to get to the spot where the Milk Saucer satellite was supposed to be positioned, and she desperately wanted to get there in one piece. After all, even though she was feeling a little better about the space walk part of her mission, she knew it would be a gigantic challenge to make sure the activation of the lifesaving satellite went off without any problems.

Bernie decided to spend some time getting to know the interior of the ship, but she tried to avoid looking at the windows that showed the vastness of outer space as much as possible as she moved around. It still creeped her out when she thought about floating around out there so far away from home.

She checked out the crew quarters, which were spare and functional, the galley, which was designed very efficiently, and the cockpit, which had carefully labeled buttons and touch screens for controlling the ship.

The last thing I want to do is bump one of those control panels, she thought. She immediately got a queasy feeling in the pit of her stomach when she thought of what a single mistake might mean. One accidental tap of a button and the ship might go off course, spinning off into an asteroid or worse—into nothing. Forever.

Mental note: Always know which direction I'm heading, Bernie thought. *No mistakes!*

Since she wasn't needed by Commander Sleek to help steer the ship, she decided to lay low until she and Jarvis had to help with launching the satellite containing the

Milk Saucer. She knew that Commander Sleek would give them plenty of time to get ready for their part of the mission so that she could suit up.

She trusted him. Sleek was all about keeping things simple.

When they'd packed for the trip, Gadget had allowed each of them to take one personal item to space. Bernie had taken a picture of her parents. But Jarvis had brought his favorite twenty-sided die and a short, two-player Mice and Dice module.

Once they figured out how to roll a twenty-sided die in zero gravity, it turned out to be a perfect way to bide the time while they had long hours with nothing to do. Jarvis was an expert at being a game master. The gangly rat was a great storyteller as he led Bernie through fun dungeons populated with all kinds of scary rat zombies and skeletal cat dragons. For a little while, Bernie even forgot they were in space because it felt so much like the fun times they'd had back at Mouse Watch HQ.

"I wish Juno was with us," Bernie said after she'd defeated a particularly nasty undead rat magician.

"Yeah, me too," said Jarvis. "She really adds a lot to our little group, doesn't she?"

Bernie nodded. "I miss her. She's always so happy!"

Jarvis rolled the die and marked down the result on a sheet. "Well, if you'd had a life like she'd had, almost anything would be better. The thing about being in the R.A.T.S. is that you can never let your guard down. There's always someone waiting to get you in trouble with the boss."

"What was he like?" asked Bernie.

"Who?"

"The boss of the R.A.T.S." said Bernie.

Jarvis shrugged. "I never saw him. In fact, most of the rodents I met were too afraid to even mention his name. They said he had eyes and ears everywhere and was ruthless if he caught you messing up. He was good at hiding, I guess." He shuddered. "I'm so glad I was only there for a short time."

"Me too, Jarvie. I hate to think of you being a part of that place."

They played the rest of the game and then, after Tony announced that it was bedtime, they both crawled into their bunks. Since it was always dark, it was impossible to know when it was day or night, but thanks to their smartwatches, they would be able to keep on schedule.

The next two days were spent much in the same way. They had regular check-ins with Sleek, but since he said that he had everything under control, they were left to do whatever they wanted. Bernie made sure to use her new goggles to take a picture of Earth for Juno. She and Jarvis played a lot of Mice and Dice. But sometimes, they broke things up by getting some exercise. Bernie discovered that the spaceship had a small workout gym. The little section in the back of the ship had a high-tech equivalent of a rotating hamster wheel that measured their vital signs while they exercised. Even Jarvis had fun with it, since running in zero gravity required much less effort. Bernie thought that it was so weird to run upside down! But she did as many laps as she could. She definitely did not want to lose the agility and speed that she'd worked so hard to develop back at HQ.

The two days passed by without much in the way of drama of any kind. But on the afternoon of the third day, things took a surprising turn. Bernie and Jarvis had just emerged from their quarters after another long session of Mice and Dice and were both feeling kind of hungry.

"Um, Commander, is it okay for us to get a snack?" asked Jarvis.

"Be my guest," said Sleek. His back was turned to them as he fiddled with some equipment on the control panel. "Just don't eat all the peanut butter, it's my favorite."

Jarvis motioned to Bernie and together, moving carefully, the two used the conveniently placed handholds on the walls and ceiling to go to the galley. Bernie was now used to how effortlessly her body glided through the air as they pulled themselves hand over hand to the kitchen section of the ship.

The snack compartment was stacked with little foil-wrapped packages. Jarvis pulled out the first one and read the label.

"Dehydrated Cheese Soufflé." He sniffed the package.

"Like you'll really smell anything," said Bernie. "You have to open it."

Jarvis tore off the label and, after a quick glance inside, popped a yellow cube into his mouth.

"Well?" asked Bernie, watching him chew.

After a gulp, Jarvis grinned. "You know what? It's not bad! The only thing that would make it better would be—"

"Here ya go!" interrupted Bernie. She handed him a small packet. "Gadget has you covered."

"Powdered Tabasco sauce!" Jarvis exclaimed happily. He ripped open the packet with his teeth and dumped some red powder into his cheese soufflé. Then, after shaking it around a little, he poured the rest of it into his mouth all at once.

Bernie didn't have a chance to stop him. She could immediately tell that downing the whole thing in one gulp was a mistake, because Jarvis was instantly seized with a coughing fit, spewing clouds of orange-and-red powder all over the galley. Worse still, because they were in space, the powder just floated there, filling the air with particles.

"Jarvis! Dude! Aaaaa-CHOOO!" Bernie said with a sneeze.

"What the Havarti?" shouted Commander Sleekwhisker. He rocketed into the galley looking furious. "Clean up this mess IMMEDIATELY!" he shouted, pointing at the cloud of dehydrated food and the discarded foil wrappers. Bernie had never seen him so mad!

Bernie went to grab a cloth from one of the drawers but was stopped by Sleek. The commander slammed the drawer shut and pointed at a small, portable vacuum that was mounted on the wall.

"Use that! And I want every speck cleaned up, is that clear?" he growled. "Use your goggles. Set the magnification to one hundred. I need you both to make ABSOLUTELY certain not a trace is left behind! Even the tiniest particle could mess up our navigation systems."

"Y-yes, sir," Bernie and Jarvis both replied.

Sleek grumbled on his way back to the cockpit as he brushed every crumb from his fastidiously clean jumpsuit. Bernie and Jarvis exchanged nervous glances. They'd never seen this side of the normally jovial commander.

"We'd better get busy," said Bernie in a hushed tone.

"Yeah," said Jarvis, glancing nervously toward Sleek.

Bernie lowered her goggles and as they flicked on, she gazed through them around the galley. The enhanced reality feature on the goggles listed descriptions next to every drawer and compartment and included little instructions for how to use each item.

"Should have put these on before," Bernie muttered. After turning on the minivac and scrupulously seeking out each and every particle, a task that was made much easier with the help of the goggles, Bernie moved to put the vacuum away when a slight flicker in the corner of her eye made her pause.

"Hey, Tony," said Bernie.

What's up? said Tony.

"Did my goggles just malfunction?" asked Bernie. "I thought I saw a flicker. Is there a glitch or something?" The thought of her goggles failing while up in space made her paws shake. They were one of her most essential items!

Let me check, said Tony. The AI was quiet for a brief moment and then replied, *Nope, nothing wrong. Everything's A-okay.*

"Weird," said Bernie. She tried turning her head back and forth, seeing if she could replicate the same flicker. As she ran her eyes past the cockpit where Sleek was sitting, the flicker happened again.

Bernie's heart froze. It wasn't a glitch with her goggles. *No, no, NO! It can't be!*

Her tail stuck out straight and stiff as a knitting needle. She knew where she'd seen that flicker before and she knew exactly what it meant.

Jarvis had just finished vacuuming his side of the galley. Bernie motioned to him, waving one paw while the other was pressed against her lips, telling him to be quiet. Looking puzzled, Jarvis set the vacuum in its holder and floated over to Bernie.

"What?" he said quietly.

Bernie moved as close as she could to Jarvis's ear and whispered, "He's not who he says he is."

"Who's not?" asked Jarvis.

Bernie pointed at the back of Commander Sleekwhisker. "Put your goggle's filter setting on high and then look."

"But that will drain the battery faster," whispered Jarvis. "I don't want to have to charge."

"Just do it," hissed Bernie.

Jarvis did as he was told. Bernie had a habit of keeping her settings on high. She loved all the extras she could see when the enhanced reality filters discovered tiny details that would have been overlooked. She'd done it ever since she'd gotten her first pair and now she was very glad that she did, even though most Watchers always had their goggles in medium or low mode.

When Jarvis looked at the big hamster, he gasped.

"That's not right," he murmured.

Bernie took the goggles back and gazed through a second time just to be sure of what she'd seen. Sure enough, the screen flickered, and then the outline of Sleek's body transformed into a completely different animal. Bernie recognized this all too well. She had seen it before, on her very first mission with the Mouse Watch. Commander Sleekwhisker—if that's who he really was—was using the holographic disguise function on his goggles. But with her own goggles set on high, she could see his true form.

The jolly commander was no hamster.

He was a rat!

CHAPTER 9

"What should we do?" asked Jarvis.

Bernie made sure the door to their quarters was locked. She and Jarvis had gone about their assigned duties without saying a word about what they'd seen. But now that it was bedtime, Sleekwhisker was in the captain's quarters and they could finally talk freely.

"We've got to think about this," Bernie said. She climbed into her bottom bunk with the magnetic blankets and pillow. Jarvis had climbed into his top bunk and was now leaning over the side, staring down at her. His blond hair hung down in a way that, ordinarily, would have made Bernie laugh. But she was too worked up to even smile.

They were trapped in space on a high-stakes mission with an imposter! Who was Commander Sleekwhisker, really?

"He's got to be a R.A.T.S. operative," said Bernie. She

couldn't help thinking about the conversation that she'd overheard back at HQ between the old mouse and the lanky agent. What if Dennis had been right to be suspicious?

"Yeah, but how could he have fooled Gadget?" Jarvis pointed out. "Whoever that really is out there, he'd have to be really good to get past her. She would never have sent someone into space with us if she couldn't trust them."

"True," said Bernie. "And I'm surprised that her goggles didn't spot the same flicker we saw. Maybe she doesn't keep her filter set on high? I don't know."

But the whole thing was weird. Back when they were training with Sleek, Bernie had used her goggles and hadn't seen anything suspicious. Why was that? Could it be that whatever tech Sleek was using to disguise himself didn't work as well when it was far from Earth? Or . . . what if his weren't even Mouse Watch–issued goggles to begin with? What if they were really, really convincing fakes?

"Remember back on our first mission?" Bernie asked. "When it turned out Digit was using the holographic disguise feature on his goggles? He was a double agent the whole time, and we never even picked up on it."

"I remember," said Jarvis. "It totally creeped me out."

Bernie had been completely fooled by the double agent that had betrayed and nearly destroyed the entire Mouse Watch.

"Man, I wish the flicker on Sleek was a little slower

so that we could see who was really under the disguise," Jarvis added. "All I could see was the outline of a rat, nothing more."

"Yeah, I know," said Bernie. "But here's the thing. If he was using the disguise function on the new goggles, he wouldn't be able to get away with it. Tony would let Gadget know what was going on. It has to be R.A.T.S. tech that just looks really, really similar to ours."

"That would be very bad," said Jarvis.

Bernie scratched her furry cheek, thinking. "Okay, so if we know he's not who he says he is, I think the next thing we should do is try to call Gadget."

Bernie half sat, half glided up in her bunk. The magnetic blankets stayed in place, but she could feel her legs levitating under the covers. Lowering her goggles, she said, "Hey, Tony, are you there?"

Always came the immediate reply.

"We need a secure line to Gadget, can you do that?" Bernie asked.

I can, but I would need special authorization from Commander Sleekwhisker, Tony replied.

"Look, Tony, can you keep a secret?"

Yeah, sure! Tony enthused. Then the tone of the AI voice changed to formal, *But if it's something classified or dangerous, I'm supposed to inform your supervisor.*

"When you say *supervisor*, you mean Gadget, right?" asked Bernie.

If she were your immediate supervisor, yes. But up here that would be Commander Sleekwhisker. Would you like me to ask him if you can make a call? Tony asked.

Bernie rubbed a frustrated paw through her hair. This wasn't going like she'd hoped. There wasn't much chance of informing Gadget about a traitor in their midst without Sleekwhisker finding out.

"That's okay," said Bernie. "I'll think about it."

She pressed the "Power Off" button on the side of the goggles and motioned for Jarvis to do the same. Taking the hint, Jarvis nodded and turned his off, too.

"We can't afford to have Tony listening in," said Bernie. "What if he tells Sleekwhisker what we're up to?"

Jarvis looked worried. "Tony might have already told him. What if he knows we know that he's an imposter?"

"If he knows that we know, then we need to keep acting like we don't know he knows that we know," said Bernie.

"Uhhhh . . ." said Jarvis, confused.

"Forget about that," Bernie said, waving her paw. "All we can do right now is to look for the right time to confront him."

Jarvis floated down out of his bunk and perched next to Bernie.

"Then we should have a code word," he said.

"How come?" asked Bernie.

"In case things go south," said Jarvis, shrugging. "Like, what if he tries to attack us? Or, if he already knows, what if he corners us one at a time when we're not expecting it?"

"I don't think we really need—" began Bernie, but Jarvis cut her off.

"The code word is *Ornithopter*," he said, folding his arms.

"Orni-whater?" asked Bernie.

"Ornithopter," said Jarvis. "In Mice and Dice it's an ancient helicopter that mouse gnome engineers can make. It's super rare."

Bernie shrugged and nodded. "Okay, fine. Ornithopter. Whatever."

She lay back on her pillow as Jarvis, looking satisfied, floated back up to his bunk. It was scary to think that there was an imposter sleeping right in the other room, not a few feet away. What did he have planned? And how could she get a message to Gadget?

After a long moment she snapped her fingers.

"Hey, Jarvie, does this ship have an onboard radio?"

"Of course. I saw it on the left side of the cockpit next to the helm controls. But how in the world could you use it without Sleek finding out?"

"I'll find a way," said Bernie. "I think it might be our best chance."

Bernie pressed a button on her smartwatch, and the lights in the cabin automatically dimmed.

Bernie stared around the room, feeling antsy. What was she waiting for? She should just try and sneak out right now and use the radio. If she was caught, she could always tell Sleekwhisker that she needed a drink of water or something.

"I'm going!" Bernie said, pulling back the magnetized covers.

"Wait, what?" said Jarvis. He popped out of his bunk so fast, his blanket came loose from its magnetic fasteners and he floated up to the ceiling. "What if he catches you?"

"I can handle it," said Bernie. "You stay here. If I'm not back in five minutes, then . . . Orni-hopper!"

"Orni-*thopter*," Jarvis corrected. His brow furrowed with concern. "Bernie, be careful, 'kay? This could be really dangerous!"

Bernie nodded. With her heart pounding, she crept over to the door. She opened it and peered into the darkened, shadowy corridor.

CHAPTER 10

The eeriness of being in a dark capsule in outer space wasn't lost on Bernie. It was downright frightening! In a weird way, knowing Sleek was in disguise was very close to the feelings she had about aliens. Here was some unknown entity, a kind of shapeshifter that was on the ship with her, all while they were hurtling through space!

It wasn't that much different than her nightmare.

Bernie gulped and tried to still her rapid breathing as she crept down the narrow hallway. She tiptoed as quietly as she possibly could past Commander Sleekwhisker's quarters. There was something so horrible about being so close to the enemy, one that was sleeping on just the other side of that door. It made the fur on her arms stand on end. She noticed that the commander's door was slightly open and couldn't help taking a stealthy peek. She had to know what was going on in there. Would the holographic disguise be off? Who—or worse, *what*—would she see when she looked inside?

Moving as soundlessly as she could, Bernie put her eye to the crack of the door and gazed inside.

The big hamster's back was to her. The room was dark and she could just make out the outline of Sleek's face. It was illuminated from below by the glow of a steady green computer screen saver on a nearby console. He was ironing one of his silver spacesuits and seemed to be muttering to himself as he drove the iron back and forth, back and forth over every single wrinkle.

Super creepy, Bernie thought.

She backed away from the door with her heart pounding. Sleekwhisker's obsessive neatness was disturbing. *Could it have something to do with keeping up his fake appearance?* Bernie wondered. She thought about Juno's instinct that Sleek wasn't all that he appeared to be.

Boy was she right!

Bernie moved quietly, even for a mouse, as she floated into the main cockpit. A bay of lights from various touch screens were on, but everything except the largest monitor—which showed a vast, star-studded sky—appeared to be in sleep mode.

Okay, now where is it? Bernie wondered.

She crept over to Sleek's station and checked all around

the console for something resembling a radio. Finally, after some stressful searching, she spotted a small box with a transmitter directly beneath a navigation computer.

Her paw had just brushed the edge of the radio's "On" switch when a light suddenly filled the cockpit.

Oh no!

Bernie barely suppressed a loud *squeak* as she dove underneath the console counter and huddled up into a ball. Thankfully, she was very small for her age and she was able to flatten herself nicely against the far wall, keeping even her toes out of sight.

From beneath the console, Bernie saw Sleekwhisker's immaculately clean white slippers float into the room. She held her breath, afraid that even the sound of her breathing would give her away.

The slippers paused next to where she was hiding. Then, to her horror, she saw Sleekwhisker's big hand reach down and turn the "On" switch on the radio transmitter she'd just been looking at moments ago. Bernie edged herself even farther into the shadows as Sleek groped for the mic, found it, and then raised it to his lips.

"K calling Lunar Base Alpha, come in."

A moment of silence. Then an answering voice crackled back, *We read you loud and clear, sir. What are your orders?*

Bernie wondered who Sleekwhisker was talking to. Who was *K*? And what was *Lunar Base Alpha*? It definitely didn't sound like a code name for Mission Control or even Mouse Watch HQ!

Lunar . . . the moon? Why did that trigger a memory? Then, all of a sudden, Bernie remembered the third point on the whiteboard presentation Sleek had given them about the mission.

The Moonshot.

At the time she'd assumed that it just meant that they had to do something really challenging. A moonshot usually meant doing something nearly impossible. But never in a million years had Bernie thought that it meant they would actually be "shooting toward" the moon as part of the mission.

"The cargo is en route. Estimated arrival, T minus twelve hours," said Sleek.

Roger that. Everything will be prepared. Congratulations, sir, came the reply.

Sleek didn't respond but instead just flicked off the radio and replaced the microphone.

As Sleekwhisker floated back to his room and shut off the light, Bernie emerged from her hiding space with her heart thudding in her chest. If there had been any doubt that something was wrong with Sleekwhisker, she was convinced now. It didn't take much thinking to figure out that the cargo was the Milk Saucer—an energy source that could save or *destroy* the world! And something told her Sleek—or whoever he was—wasn't exactly on a world-saving mission. No, the Milk Saucer was currently on a ship controlled by a traitor, hurtling through space toward a mysterious destination. And Bernie and Jarvis were hurtling right along with it. The worst part was, Gadget had no idea.

I've got to tell Jarvis, thought Bernie. *We have to do something!*

But no sooner had she crawled out from beneath the console shelf than the light suddenly flicked back on. Bernie froze. Her stomach sank as she realized she'd been caught.

"Corni-copter, Jarvis!" she shouted. That was the code word, right? "Corni-copter!"

But the code word, which she'd gotten wrong, stuck in her throat as she came face-to-face with someone she had never seen before.

It certainly wasn't Commander Sleekwhisker. It was someone else entirely—and he had Jarvis!

Floating there, holding a frightened Jarvis by the scruff of his neck, was an elegant-looking rat with immaculately brushed fur wearing a crisp white robe and matching slippers. Every article of clothing had been ironed flat and nothing, absolutely nothing, had a single stain or mark on it anywhere.

Jarvis let out a tiny, pathetic squeak. Before she could even blink, the rat moved with lightning speed to where

she stood and grabbed her the same way he had Jarvis. Bernie struggled, windmilling her arms and legs and trying to fight back, but it was no use. The rat might have been thin and elegant, but he was very, very strong.

"Well, I guess the rat's out of the bag. Allow me to introduce myself," the rat said smoothly. "My name is Kryptos."

CHAPTER 11

K*ryptos.*

Bernie knew she'd heard that name before.
But where?

She racked her brain. Had it been mentioned on one of
her missions? Had Dr. Thornpaw said it? Captain Octavia?

As the rat held her in one paw and Jarvis in the other,
Bernie felt something poking her. Glancing over, she saw
that it was Jarvis. His tail had snaked up behind her,
behind Kryptos's back.

"What are you—" she whispered.

"Shh," hissed Jarvis.

She felt the tip of his tail between her shoulder blades,
tapping out a rhythm of some kind. At first she was annoyed
and confused, but then, she suddenly realized the genius of
what he was doing.

Mouse code!

Mouse code was similar to Morse code but had been scrambled so that only members of the Watch could understand it.

Dot . . . dash . . . dash . . . dot . . . dot . . . she made a mental note of each of Jarvis's taps.

Leader . . .

Her eyes grew wide.

of . . .

Her tail went stick straight.

R.A.T.S.!

In a flash, she remembered. She'd heard the name Kryptos only once.

From Juno!

Her friend had mentioned the name right after she'd been saved by the Mouse Watch. Kryptos was Juno's old boss! She'd said that he was someone who always kept to the shadows. Someone who had led countless raids against the Watch and never got caught. A kingpin of crime who would stop at nothing less than destroying the Watch and enslaving humanity. Dr. Thornpaw and Captain Octavia, sworn enemies of the Watch, had both worked for him.

And he's right here!

Bernie struggled with the zip ties Thornpaw had wasted no time fastening around her wrists before turning his attention to the navigational controls in the cockpit. Bernie and Jarvis, in spite of their Mouse Watch hand-to-hand combat training, had been no match for his mouse-tial arts skills.

It bothered Bernie that she'd been overcome so quickly! And it bothered her even more that she hadn't seen through Kryptos's disguise earlier and done something about it sooner.

Why didn't I recognize it back at HQ? Bernie wondered. When he was disguised as Commander Sleekwhisker, hadn't he always been just a little too charming? A little *too* braggy about his many "accomplishments"? Why hadn't her Watcher's sixth sense picked up on the fact that he was a total phony?

For that matter, why hadn't Tony recognized it, too? Was it because she'd never thought to ask?

Skampersky, you're slipping, she chided herself. If only she had been wearing her smart goggles when she'd snuck out of bed, she was sure Tony could have helped her get out of this. Surely Gadget had designed Tony to recognize when Mouse Watch agents were in peril! However, she also realized that Kryptos had been intelligent enough to outsmart both Gadget and Tony.

The leader of the R.A.T.S. was more formidable than she could have ever imagined, and the scariest part about it was that he didn't look menacing at all. He looked downright . . . normal.

Bernie glanced over at Jarvis. The young rat looked

miserable. His furry face was hidden in the recesses of the hoodie that had been built into his spacesuit. Jarvis always wore a hood, and Gadget made sure that his favorite accessory was built into every article of clothing he owned, even his pajamas.

Thinking about Gadget made Bernie miss home more than ever. Here she was, stranded a million miles away from any help that the fearless leader of the Mouse Watch could offer. It was hard to fight off the feeling of despair that threatened to engulf her.

But then, Bernie noticed something, a little detail that gave her a flare of hope. She could just make out a pair of smart goggles hidden under Jarvis's hood.

If only I could find a way . . .

After waiting to make certain that Kryptos was thoroughly preoccupied with whatever he was doing in the cockpit, Bernie decided to risk a quick conversation.

"Jarvie," Bernie hissed.

"No talking!" shouted Kryptos. He wheeled around from the console and glared at both of them. "Consider yourselves my prisoners. That means you have no rights whatsoever and you must do everything I say."

"Who made you the boss?" Bernie fired back.

Kryptos looked at her for a long moment. Bernie gulped. Sometimes she had a hard time controlling her temper, and in that moment she immediately regretted it. But to her surprise, Kryptos didn't seem offended. Instead, he smiled mysteriously, then leaned back and crossed his arms.

"Who indeed?" he said quietly. "The question is a good one, although it also shows your ignorance. Since we're in space and you'll never see the inside of Mouse Watch headquarters again, I might as well tell you the truth." Bernie watched Kryptos wave his paw dismissively, as if their lives meant absolutely nothing to him.

"Gadget Hackwrench, your stupid leader, never had a chance. The Illumi-rati's influence goes far beyond just the R.A.T.S. We are a global network of shadow power. Our numbers are far, far greater than you could ever imagine. And we aren't just rodents, either! There's the Criminal Reptilian Order of Carnivores, the C.R.O.C.S. The Society of Night Assassins and Kleptomaniac Evildoers, the S.N.A.K.E.S. And the list goes on. The Mouse Watch has no idea what they're up against."

Kryptos moved closer, grinning evilly. "And as far as who made me *boss*, as you put it. Well, let's just say that it is an individual who is so powerful that with but a word, they could topple entire governments. The Mouse Watch is only left intact to serve their purposes, one of which is to retrieve and deliver the Milk Saucer into their waiting paws. The entire Illumi-rati is at their disposal."

Bernie felt all the blood drain from her face. So that was what this was all about! *So much for ending global warming,* she thought. If Kryptos and this Illumi-rati got their hands on the Milk Saucer, there might not even be a globe to save! And who was this mysterious *someone* behind all that?

"You're a monster," Bernie said through gritted teeth.

"Agreed. One that has good taste and is flawlessly well dressed," Kryptos added. Then, with a surprising gesture, he placed the tip of his finger on the end of Bernie's nose.

"Boop!" said Kryptos playfully.

That one innocent yet menacing gesture set off her temper all over again. Like a shot, Bernie dove for him. "Let me at 'em!" she squeaked, her fists flailing. "Don't you boop me! I am a member of the Mouse Watch! The most elite global crime-fighting unit on the planet!"

"Bernie, stop!" hissed Jarvis.

He's insane, Bernie thought with a shudder, but she listened to her friend. She glanced over at Jarvis, whose face was still hidden in his hood. Was he doing something with his goggles? The glance wasn't lost on Kryptos.

"Ah, yes, that little detail." Kryptos pulled back Jarvis's hood and removed the goggles that were perched on his forehead. "Wouldn't have mattered anyway. Tony has been turned off."

"Wait, what?" exclaimed Jarvis. "That can't be done. It's a secure program."

"Not when you've been voice authorized as a Level Ten Mouse Watch agent and commander of a top secret space mission," said Kryptos. "One word from me that the safety of the mission had been compromised, and POOF!" He waved his paw. "Bye-bye, Tony."

Bernie felt a nauseating sense of doom settle in her stomach. It really looked like there would be no way for her and Jarvis to get out of this dilemma. There was no way to call for backup. No chance of Gadget sending a troop of Mouse Watch agents to save the day. They were stuck up in space in a little tin can with a megalomaniac supervillain.

"Wh-what are you going to do with us?" Bernie asked quietly.

Kryptos glanced at his watch. Bernie noticed that he still wore his regulation Mouse Watch smartwatch, the same one all agents wore. It seemed like a betrayal of everything she believed in to see it on his wrist. The Mouse Watch stood for everything Kryptos was against.

"Soon, we'll be arriving at my secret moon base, where I will deliver the Milk Saucer into the hands of my top scientists. The use I have for it will not be"—he stopped to chuckle, then continued—"to aid humanity. No, what I have planned will catapult the Illumi-rati out from the shadows and into the public. A new world will emerge, one that I can assure you will be most unpleasant to your Mouse Watch colleagues."

"But . . . but what about us?" Jarvis squeaked.

"You? Oh, I have something very special in mind for the two young agents that so nearly spoiled my plans." Kryptos paused dramatically, cracking his long-knuckled rat paws and staring gleefully down at his two prisoners.

"You will have the distinct honor of being the very first mouse prisoners on the moon. You'll be left there forever while I, and my minions, return to Earth to execute my greatest plan."

His laugh was so horrible and so sinister that, if Bernie had been watching it in a movie, it would have been funny. But it wasn't, because it was real life.

Bernie could tell that Kryptos was laughing with real pleasure at the thought of the misfortune that he was about to bring upon her, and it sent horrified chills running up and down her spine. Bernie truly wondered if this time there would be no escape and she and Jarvis would end up growing old in a prison cell hundreds of thousands of miles away from home.

Could this really mean the end of everything she knew and loved?

CHAPTER 12

The glowing, pockmarked surface of the moon filled the entire view screen. Bernie watched, both fascinated and terrified. It was something she'd seen a million times from the comfort of Earth. The moon she'd looked up at from Thousand Acorns when she was a kid was the same moon she trained under as a Level Two agent of the Mouse Watch. It had always seemed impossibly far away. And now, they were hurtling toward it at breakneck speed.

Kryptos had said that this was where she would spend the rest of her life, rotting miles and miles from everything she held dear. She thought of the mysterious question mark floating in space on Sleekwhisker's mission diagram, and shuddered.

Not if I can help it, Bernie thought with determination.

There just had to be a way to escape before she met the most horrible fate she could have ever imagined.

The capsule made its slow, precise descent and touched down next to the South Pole–Aitken basin, the largest crater on the far side of the moon.

When the landing gear met the surface and plumes of moon dust rose in a cloud from the impact, a shudder ran through both the ship and Bernie's spine. They were really on the moon!

"All right, you two, time to go," said Kryptos.

Bernie saw that he'd retrieved the Milk Saucer from the satellite. The saucer was a glowing, Frisbee-shaped disc and Kryptos had it safely tucked underneath one arm. Bernie stared at the amazing artifact, remembering how proud she'd been to bring the device home, especially after everything she and Jarvis had gone through to get it. But now . . . now she wished it had never come into her life at all.

Having no choice but to obey, Bernie and Jarvis rose from their seats and, with their paws still tightly bound behind them, descended the ramp.

At least we have helmets on, she thought. *He could have just as easily pushed us out and then we would have died immediately without air!*

But in some ways, Bernie realized that Kryptos was just delaying the torture to come. In her worst nightmares about going to outer space, being left in a prison on the moon while her captor flew back to Earth had never occurred to her.

If it had, Bernie would have most certainly woken up screaming.

They half marched, half floated in silence as Kryptos urged them toward a low, flat building that was half hidden by the massive crater's edge. Bernie had wondered how such a thing could have gone unnoticed by human scientists, but as they drew close, she noticed how carefully camouflaged the moon base was, how it was designed to mostly look like just another rugged part of the moon surface.

Bernie glanced at Jarvis. Through the glass in his mousetronaut helmet she could see the worry etched on his furry face.

Poor Jarvie! He finally got to go to the moon and he can't even enjoy it.

The big vacuum doors of the R.A.T.S. secret moon base opened with a loud, wheezing *groan*. Bernie and Jarvis were shoved through, and as the hydraulic doors shut behind them, a second set opened, letting in a flow of oxygenated air.

"Hey!" shouted Bernie as she felt her helmet roughly taken.

"Won't be needing that anymore," said a high-pitched, raspy voice. It belonged to a R.A.T.S. agent, a scruffy thing with large clumps of hair missing all over its lumpy head. It laughed, noticing Bernie's look of helpless anger.

"Get them to the cells, SnotTooth," said Kryptos. "And see to it they're imprisoned separately. I don't want them getting any ideas about escaping."

"Yes, sir, of course, sir," SnotTooth groveled. He seized Jarvis and Bernie by the collars of their jumpsuits and shoved them roughly ahead.

Bernie glanced around, noting the massive size of the secret base. It wasn't fancy and futuristic looking. Nothing like Gadget would have designed. The overall effect was one of simple functionality with haphazard attention to detail. It reminded her of buildings she'd seen on MouseTube in footage of communist Russia. Gray, bleak, and suited to only the most perfunctory needs.

It was, however, also one of the biggest warehouses Bernie had ever seen. It was filled from ceiling to floor with towering scaffolds and heavy-duty machinery.

What's it all for? Bernie wondered. And more importantly, how was it that the Mouse Watch had never known about it? Could it be that Kryptos really was smarter and one step ahead of Gadget? Had the R.A.T.S. been running secret missions to the moon for ages?

She soon found out.

As the prisoners rounded the corner, Bernie gasped.

Stretching out ahead of them in the echoing warehouse, an army of huge, mechanical rat soldiers stood at the ready. The massive robots were easily as tall as thirty rats standing on each other's shoulders and stretched as far as her eye could see. Assembling an army like that would have required unimaginable effort. The R.A.T.S. had obviously been building an attack plan for years and years, and somehow they'd managed to slip it right past the Mouse Watch.

Bernie's stomach sank down to her knees and her paws shook. How had they managed to fool her hero, Gadget Hackwrench? Up until that moment, she'd truly believed Gadget to be practically infallible.

Do the good guys always win? she wondered. *What if we've just been lucky?*

And, as if the robot army wasn't bad enough, Bernie saw something that made her gasp with horror.

Big cranes were transporting R.A.T.S. agents from a long table filled with jars, each of which had a floating brain inside of it. Once the agent grabbed the jar, they were lifted high up to the robotic heads where they proceeded to place the brains inside.

If Bernie hadn't seen it with her own eyes, she would have never believed it.

He's using rat brains in each of those giant robots!

Kryptos was creating a horrific fusion of living tissue

and mechanical pistons, gears, tanks, and hydraulics. He'd created a massively powerful army of obedient soldiers that would execute his every sinister command. She noticed that etched on the shoulders of each one of the mechanical monsters was a strange symbol, a pyramid-shaped eye with a slotted pupil inside of it. A series of lightning bolts shot out from around it, seeming to indicate that the eye was omnipresent.

The Illumi-rati, she thought. She shuddered involuntarily, feeling a renewed sense of horror at the thought of the evil shadow empire.

Bernie thought back to when she'd faced Dr. Thornpaw, a lab rat who had replaced his injured body parts with super-enhanced, robotic replacements. Was that where Kryptos had gotten the idea? Had he pitched the idea of cyborg rat hybrids to his dark masters and they'd seen to it that the entire operation was hidden from even the most sensitive spy gear the Mouse Watch had to offer?

It was a horrible thought.

SnotTooth, noticing the looks of revulsion on Bernie's and Jarvis's faces, cackled, the laugh escaping his ragged throat like a long hiss.

"Impossible? Won't work, you think?" SnotTooth grinned, exposing broken yellow teeth. "Many rats gave up their lives to become super soldiers. And now that the boss has the Milk Saucer, they will be stronger than they ever were before. They can go and go and go and never stop! They will live forever!" The laugh that followed sent the ugly rat into convulsive coughs.

Bernie realized the full extent of Kryptos's plan. This was why he'd needed the Milk Saucer so badly. It would take a tremendous source of power to make such things capable of life and movement, and the Milk Saucer was just that. He really was like Dr. Frankenstein, unleashing his terrible creations on the world.

How can the Watch ever win against that? We don't stand a chance!

It was the last thought she had as she was shoved roughly into a dungeonlike cell.

Bernie banged on the door. She shouted to be let free. She would have tried to pick the lock, but everything, all her Watcher gear, had been taken from her.

With a sinking feeling, she realized that this time, the R.A.T.S. had truly won and she was absolutely powerless to stop them.

Bernie huddled into a ball in the corner of her cell. She gazed around with wide, terrified eyes. Her whiskers trembled. Then, feeling absolutely hopeless and defeated, she began to cry for the first time since joining the Mouse Watch.

Feeling absolutely alone and more terrified than she'd ever felt, Bernie Skampersky eventually fell asleep on the cold metal cot. For the first time in a long while, her sleep was empty and untroubled by nightmares.

Because now, in her waking world, she was living one.

CHAPTER 13

Bernie woke to the sound of thunder.

As she cracked her eyelids open, she saw a flash of blue light through the narrow window in her cell door. The ground beneath her shook. Bernie stumbled out of her metal cot and rushed to the window for a better look. In the giant hangar, the R.A.T.S. super-soldiers were taking off like rockets, blue fire blasting from their mechanical feet. The dome above them had been opened, revealing a sky strewn with stars.

At the same time, they lifted off into the air, rising slowly and ominously. Bernie's eyes were still red and puffy from crying, but they narrowed in anger when she saw that Kryptos had stolen the USS *Mozzarella* and was using it to lead his flying army of rat-brained robots.

It was a heart-wrenching sight. And she was watching it all happen from a jail cell, powerless to stop it.

There they go . . . she thought angrily. *And with them, all hopes for humanity and rodentkind.*

Bernie shuffled back to her cot and slumped down upon it. Sighing, she glanced at the one meal she'd been given—a hard crust of stale bread and a half glass of murky-looking water.

This whole situation seemed surreal, as if she were in a dream. Bread and water and not even a crumb of cheese. Would it be the last food she would ever have? How in the world had she gotten here?

Bernie wished she could talk to Jarvis, but there didn't seem any way to communicate. The cell walls were so thick they were probably soundproof. Thankfully, her prison was oxygenated. But Bernie had no idea how long it would be before that ran out. Were there any R.A.T.S. agents left behind to guard the base?

Had they all been able to hitch a ride back to Earth on one of the giant robots?

Were she and Jarvis the *only* living beings on the moon?

Going back to the window, Bernie scanned the room where the giant robots had just been, but she couldn't see a single sign of life.

Her heart began to race.

The feeling of isolation that she'd always feared she would experience in space came rushing back. She'd been able to keep it at bay when she knew that at least there were others around, even if they were enemies, and that maybe, just maybe, she'd be able to find a way out of her cell.

Her breathing came in short gasps. Flashes of all the nightmares she'd ever had about being lost in space flooded her mind. Lights flashed before her eyes and the room began to spin.

She was having a panic attack!

I gotta get out of here!

"I think I can help you with that," said a quiet voice.

Bernie wheeled around. "Who said that?" she demanded. Then, with a creepy feeling she realized that the voice she'd just heard had responded to something that she hadn't said out loud.

Something had read her thoughts!

Slowly, like a blurry picture coming into focus, a shape emerged in her cell. It seemed to seep from the shadows near the back wall and then to slowly materialize, melting into existence.

Bernie felt a scream well up in her throat. The only other thing she'd feared, possibly worse than being isolated in space, was something from another world. Was it a ghost? Or worse, an *alien*?

Bernie felt her knees turn to water and the world around her fade.

And just as the weird, otherworldly creature solidified before her, she fainted.

CHAPTER 14

Bernie awoke to see a concerned, fuzzy face looking down at her. Feeling disoriented, at first she thought she was back at Mouse Watch HQ. But then, as her vision came into focus, she noticed that the mouse staring down at her had fur that was tinged green.

"Freen?" the mouse said.

"Who . . . what . . . are you?" Bernie stammered.

She was talking with an alien! A *mouse* alien! There was no other explanation. But, where had he come from and how had he gotten into her cell?

"AAAAAAAH!" screamed Bernie. Without sparing the creature a second glance, she leapt up and rushed to the cell door. "HELLLP!" she yelled, pounding on it in the hopes that someone, anyone, would hear her. No one came.

It was only after two solid minutes of screaming,

pounding, and clawing at the door that she realized the creature hadn't made a sound, or moved to attack. In fact, when she turned and hazarded a tiny peek at it over her shoulder, she saw that it hadn't even moved. It just stood there, smiling at her.

Staring at his friendly little face, she had to admit, he didn't look anything like the frightening images that had haunted her ever since she was little.

"You . . . you're not going to melt my brain, are you?" asked Bernie, thinking of one particularly horrifying scene in the movie her brother had made her watch.

The little mouse made a funny gurgling noise in his throat and shook his head no. Did he understand her?

The green mouse was a little smaller than she was— which was saying a lot because she was the smallest mouse at the Watch. He was actually kind of cute! Like a little green baby mouse, but with sharp, intelligent eyes that showed he was clearly an adult.

"Do you . . . have a name?" she asked tentatively.

The strange mouse took a moment before answering Bernie's question. Bernie thought he looked like he was trying to understand her language. A moment later, a dawning realization made him smile and he said in a halting, heavily accented voice:

"I V'ELVEETA. From Planet Veet. I . . . freen."

Bernie scrunched up her nose, trying to understand.

The mouse seemed to know that she was confused. Lifting a gloved paw, he motioned in the air. Bernie gaped as a holographic image of the galaxy appeared out of nowhere. A single star was circled and highlighted in the floating projection.

"Veet," said the mouse, pointing at the star.

"Is that the name of your home planet?" asked Bernie.

"Plooplefoot!" exclaimed the mouse happily.

"Huh?" asked Bernie.

"Plooplefoot. Mean . . . uh . . ." The mouse screwed up his face in concentration for a minute and then said, "Mean, very . . . good!" He was picking up on English remarkably fast for someone from another planet.

"Wow. Plooplefoot," said Bernie in awe.

The little green mouse smiled and nodded.

"So, how did you get in my cell? Can you walk through walls?"

"Ploop," said the mouse.

"Ploop?"

"Er . . . yes," said Velveeta. "Walk through walls." He gestured at the door. Then, to demonstrate, his form shimmered and took on that weird melty quality that Bernie had seen earlier. First he grew into an insubstantial blob, then he floated over to the thick metal door and disappeared right through it. He came back through a second later and melted back into three-dimensional form.

"Whoa!" said Bernie.

"Po," agreed Velveeta.

The realization hit Bernie that she was actually having a conversation with a real-life alien. She took in his green, shimmery space suit and purple gloves, both made of a shiny, metallic fabric. The dark green suit accented his light green fur, and she wondered, absently, if he had become that color from eating green cheese.

What if the moon is made of it after all? she thought. And then had to stifle a hysterical giggle. All in all, this encounter was absolutely NOTHING like the horror she'd imagined upon meeting an alien.

"Hey, Velveeta, can I ask a favor?" she ventured.

"Ploop?" replied the mouse.

"Is there any way you can help me escape? My friend is locked in another cell and the Rogue Animal Thieves Society is on its way to destroy my planet!"

This was a lot for Velveeta to take in, even for an alien who seemed to be able to read her thoughts and understand her language. The alien mouse processed the long sentence for a bit before smiling and nodding.

"Ploop! Take . . . my . . . eeble, freen."

"Um. What's a feeble? Or a . . . freen?" asked Bernie.

"Feeble. This." He held out his gloved paw. "Freen . . . er . . . um . . ."

He thought a minute, then brightened. "Friend."

"Oh. Friend. And you mean take your, ah, your *paw*. Okay," said Bernie. She did as he asked. Before she had time to wonder what to do next, she saw the world around her grow hazy and indistinct. Looking down, she saw that her body had melted in the same way that the alien mouse's had moments before.

This is crazy, thought Bernie. And it didn't even hurt one bit.

Velveeta led her over to the metal wall. It felt completely unnatural to Bernie to float straight up to the door and, instead of stopping, keep going right through it! Going through the door felt just like walking through ordinary air except for the *bloopy* sound that was made as they both turned into globulous goo for a split second.

When they were on the other side, Velveeta let go and Bernie felt herself return to normal. Bernie stared around, hardly able to believe she was on the outside of her cell. In a matter of seconds she'd gone from believing that there would never be any hope to suddenly feeling like she actually had a chance. Maybe, with a little luck and some help from an alien mouse, she and Jarvis might find a way to stop Kryptos!

Thankfully, there didn't seem to be many R.A.T.S. agents about. Bernie couldn't tell if every one of them had boarded the giant rocket mice back to Earth or not, but she had a feeling that most of them had gone and left the base empty.

It only took a moment to find Jarvis's cell, since it was right on the other side of the wall from Bernie's. Velveeta did his trick, and the two of them melted into existence in front of Jarvis, who promptly screamed and dove underneath his metal bunk, dropping something behind him with a clatter on the hard cement floor.

"Jarvie, it's me!" exclaimed Bernie. Given his size, it was impressive that he'd managed to squeeze himself underneath the narrow space beneath the bunk. At Bernie's voice, Jarvis peeked out from under the bed with wide, frightened eyes.

"How do I know it's really you?" he squeaked.

"It's me," said Bernie, deadpan. "Who else would it be?"

Jarvis narrowed his eyes and looked at her suspiciously. "That's exactly what a body-snatching alien would say."

Okay, so this is weird, thought Bernie. *Now Jarvis is as freaked out about aliens as I was!*

"Would an alien know that you spilled powdered Tabasco sauce on the USS *Mozzarella* and made yourself sneeze?"

Jarvis thought for a minute. "What if you can read my mind?"

"Jarvie, we don't have time for this," said Bernie.

"Kryptos took off for Earth with those giant mecha rats. If we don't stop him, he might destroy the entire planet! You're just going to have to trust me!"

Jarvis considered this, then seemed convinced. With much grunting and straining, he managed to unwedge himself from under the bunk bed. When he saw Velveeta, his eyes grew wide.

"Okay, wow. Who's the little green guy and how did you both just appear like that?"

"That's Velveeta. He's an alien and he's *not* what I thought one would be like. At all," she added.

"Whoa," said Jarvis.

"Exactly," said Bernie.

Glancing over at him, Bernie saw that Velveeta was acting really weird. He was staring at the thing Jarvis had dropped earlier, which she now saw was a red twenty-sided die from Mice and Dice. Velveeta had an odd reverential expression on his face, almost like he was looking at some kind of holy relic.

Trying to be helpful, Bernie walked over and picked it up so that the little green mouse could look at it more closely. Velveeta immediately backed away with an awe-struck expression.

"It's a die," said Bernie. "It's for an Earth game. You can hold it if you want to," she said. But when she tried to hand it to him, Velveeta wouldn't take it.

Jarvis walked over and took the die from Bernie. "It's okay," he said soothingly. "I just brought it with me as a good luck charm. It's not dangerous. . . ." He rolled it on the ground.

"A natural twenty!" exclaimed Jarvis, noticing that the die had landed on that number. "That's a great roll!"

Whatever Bernie had expected Velveeta's response to be, she hadn't expected the little mouse to let out a loud "WHOOP!" and to begin dancing a crazy jig right there on the spot, waving his paws above his head and stomping his feet. As the little green alien pranced and jumped, Bernie and Jarvis burst out laughing. They had no idea why he was acting the way he was, but Velveeta looked like he was having the greatest moment of his life over the outcome of a die roll!

"Jarvie?"

"Yeah?"

"I don't think I'll ever have a nightmare about aliens again," Bernie said with a chuckle.

CHAPTER 15

It took some doing, but with a lot of effort, Bernie and Jarvis finally found out what was making the little mouse so happy.

"So wait, so you're telling us that the die is magic?" asked Jarvis.

"Not . . . magic. Foopynoopy," said Velveeta seriously.

"*Foopynoopy.* Does that mean . . . 'special' or something?" asked Bernie.

The green mouse beamed up at her. "Special. Yes. My home . . . need . . . Foopynoopy . . . die . . ." He screwed up his face in concentration, trying to figure out the right words to say. "Gem of Twenty . . . Numbers . . . will help V'El Veeta's fellows. It is a . . . prophecy . . ."

"I think he's saying that this die is linked to, like, some kind of prophecy," said Bernie.

"Is he?" questioned Jarvis. "Maybe they just have a

game and they lost their die and haven't been able to get a new one."

Bernie felt that it was practically impossible to tell. All she knew was that the little mouse seemed to really need it and maybe if they helped him, he would help them as well.

"Velveeta, you can have this Gem of Twenty Numbers if you'll help us, okay?" said Bernie.

"But that's my lucky—" began Jarvis.

Bernie silenced him with a look that said, *It's either that or be stuck in moon jail forever.* Jarvis got the message.

Velveeta looked at both of them hopefully.

"You'll help?" asked the mouse.

"Yes, er, *ploop!*" said Bernie. "Jarvis and I need to get back to our planet. To Earth. If we give you the die, will you take us to Earth?"

It took a minute, but it seemed that the more Bernie spoke with the little alien, the quicker he understood their language. She wondered if this alien was able to process languages much faster than humans and Earth mice. After all, he did seem to read her mind earlier. Maybe he had some kind of telepathic or psychic abilities.

"Prophecy come true! Yes!" said Velveeta. "But I take you to my home first. Show die."

"Okay, but we're in a big hurry," said Bernie. "How fast can we get to your planet?"

Velveeta grinned. *"Zorpizim!"* he said. "My ship fast. Come. Take feeble."

He held out his paws. Bernie motioned for a confused looking Jarvis to hold the little mouse's paws. Seconds later they'd passed through Jarvis's cell door and were following Velveeta through the huge, domed launchpad where the giant robots had been earlier.

"How did he get here?" asked Jarvis as they trotted after him.

"My question is *why* is he here? Did the R.A.T.S. capture him?"

"If so, they weren't very good at holding him prisoner," said Jarvis, then added, "I don't think anybody *could* hold him prisoner, actually."

They turned a corner and Bernie nearly ran into Velveeta's back. The little alien had stopped suddenly and was pointing at a group of R.A.T.S. agents at the end of the long, doorless corridor. Fortunately, their backs were turned or they would have spotted Velveeta, Bernie, and Jarvis for sure.

"What do we do? They're blocking the only way out!" whispered Jarvis anxiously.

"Feeble," said Velveeta.

"Feeble," agreed Bernie, taking his paw and extending hers to Jarvis.

"No idea what that means, but okay," said Jarvis, holding on to her.

The three shimmered into amorphous, melty, almost invisible blobs. If the R.A.T.S. agents happened to look their way, they'd just see some shiny floating moon goo.

And at first, it seemed like that was exactly what would happen.

As they drew close, Bernie saw one of the agents turn and stare at them with a wide-eyed look of terror. He pointed at them, wagging his finger, barely able to make a sound. The two other agents next to him turned around and froze in fear at the sight of the floating Bernie, Jarvis, and Velveeta.

But it only lasted a second.

Perhaps it was because of their training, or maybe it was because they were terrified, but all three immediately produced metal rods from holsters on their backs. Each rod was wired to a 9-volt battery, and one look at them told Bernie the kind of damage they would do. Gadget's tech was, of course, in most ways far superior to most of what the R.A.T.S. fought with. But it didn't take a genius to see that those battery-powered shocking sticks would be painful and maybe even deadly.

Snarling, the R.A.T.S. soldiers advanced, waving their sticks menacingly at the floating blobs that were coming toward them. Bernie didn't know what to do. They had no way to defend themselves.

But she also didn't know what little Velveeta was capable of. She felt the grip on her paw release and the three of them melted back into view. As soon as the R.A.T.S. saw that they were facing not three supernatural beings but two prisoners that Kryptos had put them under strict orders to keep locked up (and also a green mouse), they let out a great shout and charged.

Bernie and Jarvis both assumed defensive karate stances. Bernie hoped that her mouse-tial arts training against weapons would be enough to keep her from getting electrocuted. But she needn't have worried.

Velveeta was more than a match for the R.A.T.S.

The alien's cute dark eyes suddenly glowed with green fire. Then a strange look came over each of the R.A.T.S. agents. They froze, and their eyes slowly changed to mirror the glowing green in Velveeta's eyes. They stood as still as statues.

"How did he—" began Jarvis.

"Shh . . ." whispered Bernie. "We don't want to break his concentration."

Bernie and Jarvis followed as the little mouse led them past the stupefied guards. Right after they passed, Velveeta made a little flicking motion with his paw. No sooner had he made that motion than the three guards began robotically walking in the other direction, back down the hall that they'd just come from. In the distance, there was the sound of the cell doors clanking shut as they locked themselves inside, as prisoners.

"Amazing," breathed Jarvis. Turning to Velveeta, he asked, "Where did you come from, little guy?"

"Velveeta go too far from . . . home," he said with a shrug. "Ship run out of vroom. Blooie! Land on moon."

With the little mouse leading them, they had no trouble dodging the next series of guards. But as soon as they went through a final door into a large, hangarlike area, Bernie noticed signs of strain on the little mouse's face. His glowing green eyes flickered, like a lightbulb that was about to go out, and little beads of sweat were appearing on his muzzle.

Feeling worried, Bernie glanced in front of them and saw that there were about a dozen guards lounging about. But it was what was *behind* them that made her eyes widen with surprise. There, looking like something from a bad science-fiction movie, was a round silver spaceship.

A *real flying saucer!* thought Bernie.

At first, it looked like Velveeta's mind control power was going to work, that they would be able to get to his ship safely and without confrontation. But unfortunately, Velveeta suddenly faltered and bent over double, breathing hard.

"A-are you okay?" asked Bernie, putting her paw on his shoulder.

"Slorcha . . . slorcha . . ." he mumbled, then fainted with the green glow fading from his eyes.

"No!" said Bernie.

Her shout seemed to break the guards' trance. Suddenly alert, they spotted the escaped prisoners.

"GET THEM!"

Bernie and Jarvis wasted no time. Fortunately, Velveeta was very light. They had no trouble carrying the little mouse between them as they raced as fast as they could toward the alien ship.

Bernie and Jarvis saw the opening at the same time. But she knew that it was going to be close. The rats were gaining on them with terrific speed. Electricity crackled up and down their shock sticks as they ran, howling with rage at the escapees.

Thirty feet.

Twenty feet.

Ten.

Five.

Bernie and Jarvis both raced up the ramp to the saucer's open door. As they leapt inside, there was a loud *ZAP!*

Jarvis let out a *YELP!*

And Bernie smelled burning fur.

But then they were inside the saucer and the door closed automatically behind them, trapping the R.A.T.S. on the other side.

"Ow, ow, ow, OW!" shouted Jarvis. The two dropped Velveeta between them. Jarvis wiggled his injured

hindquarters on the floor of the ship, squirming with discomfort from the shock of the weapon.

"Are you all right?" Bernie asked him.

Jarvis inspected his leg. "It's not so bad. What about him?"

Bernie perched over Velveeta. She stared anxiously down at him and said softly, "Hey . . . hey, are you okay? Wake up, little guy."

He didn't move. But because she could see his chest rising and falling, at least Bernie knew that the worst hadn't happened.

"What do we do now?" asked Jarvis while rubbing his leg.

"I don't know," admitted Bernie. She could hear the rat guards outside, banging their metal rods against the sides of the ship.

Thankfully, it didn't seem to have an effect.

"Boolga bazeeba?" came a quiet voice.

Bernie looked down and was surprised to see Velveeta's black, marblelike eyes staring back up at her.

"I'm . . . A . . . o . . . kay!" he said, holding up his little gloved paw in a thumbs-up.

Bernie couldn't resist giving him a hug. The little alien seemed surprised by the gesture, but didn't complain.

"The R.A.T.S. are trying to get in," said Bernie. "What do we do now?"

The small green mouse got to his feet. He waddled quickly over to the ship's control panel and pressed his paw to a black, featureless dashboard that lit up instantly upon contact. A small window opened and a tentacle emerged. It roped up toward Velveeta's mouth, and Bernie realized it was a weird-looking microphone. He leaned into it and spoke.

"Grooble! Banbeeza shupu!"

Bernie felt the ship instantly lift from the ground. A view screen appeared, showing the R.A.T.S. guards who had crawled up onto the surface of the ship go sliding off, shouting as they fell.

"Wait, how are we gonna get out of the hangar?" asked Jarvis. "There's no exit!"

A green beam shot out of the front of the ship, evaporating a large part of the moon-base wall. Unfortunately for the remaining R.A.T.S. guards, the sudden loss of pressurized oxygen sucked them right out of the opening and into the vacuum of space. Velveeta guided his ship through the opening after them.

Contoured seats appeared beneath her and Jarvis, sliding into position without a sound. Then, before either of them could say a word about how relieved they were to be making an escape, all three were zooming through the vast, star-studded galaxy in an alien spacecraft and leaving what had seemed like an inescapable prison far, far behind them.

CHAPTER 16

"Juno will never believe this," said Jarvis as he stared at the big green planet in the view screen. "I told her that the truth was out there and she never, ever believed me. I can't wait to tell her I was right."

Bernie chuckled. How was it that just an hour or two before she'd been convinced that neither of them would ever be back on Earth, playing Mice and Dice again.

"Yeah," said Bernie. "But we still have to get back home and stop Kryptos and his Illumi-rati. If we don't hurry his robots will start taking over the world and it will be too late!"

She kept the anxious thought inside, reminding herself not to give up hope. After all the recent, seemingly impossible things that had happened, she needed to keep her faith strong in the belief that they would find a way back in time.

If I escaped that moon prison, then I should never lose heart again, she thought. For the first time in a long while she allowed herself a deep, calming breath.

Somehow, she would get through this and then together, she and Jarvis would find a way to stop Kryptos.

After orbiting a strange orange planet with three rings around it, the glittering metal saucer descended through some pink clouds and hovered low in the middle of a very unusual city. At first, Bernie couldn't figure out why it all looked familiar. There were markings on the ground below them that looked like a huge grid. Had she seen it in a sci-fi movie somewhere? It made her think of something, but she couldn't quite put her paw on why it looked so familiar. . . .

Positioned along the grid were high, mazelike walls and tall turrets. Then, with a snap of her paws, she suddenly knew where she'd seen it all before.

"Hey! I know what this looks like!" exclaimed Jarvis. He turned to Bernie with an amazed grin on his furry face.

"Mice and Dice!" they both said at the same time.

Now that she saw it up close, it was uncanny how the entire space city resembled their favorite role-playing game. The ground was covered with a glowing grid, and the buildings floated a few inches above it, as if they could be moved around like game pieces.

"How is that even possible?" exclaimed Jarvis.

"I don't know, but it's so cooool," said Bernie. "It's like actually being in the game!"

Bernie had no idea how this alien culture, which was so far from Earth, could have even known about Mice and Dice! Nowhere in the star-studded sky did she see any sign of her home planet.

"It's totally surreal," she murmured.

As the ship gently descended for a landing, she could see creatures that resembled Velveeta. Even the aliens were wearing outfits that were eerily similar to descriptions of the game characters that Bernie and Jarvis had played themselves.

Bernie never imagined that her first encounter with an alien culture would have been anything like this. If she had, she would have been excited to go to space!

Bernie practically danced in anticipation as the door slid open, but Jarvis instinctively held his breath and wrapped his paws around his nose and mouth.

"Might not be oxygen," he said in a nasally voice. "Quick, cover all breathing holes!"

Bernie ignored him, instead taking a deep breath, sniffing the strange, slightly metallic-smelling air.

"It smells a little . . . like stinky cheese . . . but seems fine to me!" Bernie shrugged, then happily followed Velveeta as he marched down the gangplank. Jarvis, after carefully taking a suspicious testing breath for himself, trotted behind.

As they drew closer to the game board, Bernie was amazed to see the game play in action. The alien mice, after pressing a glowing green gem fastened to their belts, could shape-shift into any form needed in the game. She watched as a mouse dressed as an elf princess shimmered and suddenly became a Level Ten Rat Zombie Lich Lord, a monster she knew all too well from countless tries at beating it.

"This is amazing!" she said.

Velveeta nodded proudly. "Mice . . . and . . . Dice. It is our favorite pastime. We play game every day. Before game . . . very boring life on planet. Our scout ship landed on Earth in the year nineteen hundred and eighty. We . . . take game as souvenir, but it make big problem."

Bernie was happy to see that the more time they spent together, the better Velveeta was getting at communicating in English.

"What's the big problem?" asked Jarvis. "To me, it looks like a dream come true!"

"We have no dice! No Gem of Twenty Numbers! When

we take the game so long, long ago we lose instructions and die."

Bernie saw two of the aliens square off on different spots of the board. The first one rolled a blank white cube. Because no numbers showed up, neither of them knew what to do, so they just started battling with each other, the wizard shooting fireballs and the paladin swinging a big silver ax.

Fortunately, Bernie realized that the weapons that the two players used didn't cause any real damage. Whenever the ax came close to hitting, the other alien mouse simply melted for a quick second and the blade passed right through.

"But I don't get it," said Jarvis, scratching his head. "Where's the fun in this?"

"Ploop! Yes!" said Velveeta enthusiastically. "No fun! Just hard work all day until players are exhausted. We've been playing for many turns and everybody is worn out."

Bernie had always wondered about the differences between alien cultures and her own. She'd seen plenty of sci-fi shows depicting superior civilizations and creepy monsters. But never, ever, in her wildest dreams would she have imagined that somewhere up in space was a strange culture of alien mice playing Mice and Dice without a twenty-sided die!

"Okay, well, now that you have the Gem of Twenty Numbers, how about you start playing by the rules?"

"The rules?" asked Velveeta, his face lighting up. "You know the instructions?" He began to chatter excitedly. "The prophecy is true!"

And before they could say anything in response, Velveeta ran out onto the massive game board and shouted in his alien tongue.

When he finished, a hush fell over the furry green mice. They stared at the newcomers with awe and respect. After a long, awkward pause, Jarvis raised the red twenty-sided die into the air and showed it to the mass gathering.

A deafening cheer arose from the crowd.

Bernie watched as a hulking emerald dragon shimmered and transformed back into a particularly regal-looking mouse who wore a silver band on her head. Her long green robes trailed behind her as she approached Bernie and Jarvis.

Bernie was reminded of another royal figure that she'd met, Empress Fluffyface. The massive cat was the leader of Catlantis and held herself with the same regal bearing. But that's where the comparison ended. Bernie noticed that besides the physical differences, this alien mouse radiated something warmer. She was less aloof than Fluffyface, and when she spread her arms wide and smiled, Bernie couldn't help smiling back.

She reminds me of my grandma!

"Freens," she began. "Mapoople ziphun, charkle panswobble . . ."

Fortunately, Velveeta was there to translate. "This is our queen, Her Royal Majesty Madrigal the Magnificent. She says, *Friends, you are very welcome. You have fulfilled the prophecy and we couldn't be more happy to see you.*"

The queen continued speaking, and Velveeta translated as quickly as he was able to. Bernie and Jarvis waited for her to finish each sentence so that Velveeta could help them understand.

"You have given us a great gift of the Gem of Twenty Sides," Velveeta translated for Queen Madrigal. "If you will please also tell us instructions on how to play game, then we only ask how we can repay such kindness. Anything I have in my kingdom is yours for the asking. Make yourselves at home."

And those were the words that Bernie had been hoping to hear. Stepping forward, she bowed to the queen and said, "Your Majesty, we ask that you might help us in a time of great need. The evil creatures that imprisoned us are on their way to destroy our home planet. If you could help us, we would be forever grateful."

Velveeta translated Bernie's speech and, when he was done, the queen smiled and clapped her paws together once. Velveeta turned to Bernie and said, "She agrees.

After you explain to us the rules of Mice and Dice, we will help you. She also wonders if you would like a . . ." Velveeta's face screwed up in concentration for a minute as he searched for the right translation word. "I think the word is . . . a *cookie?*"

Bernie and Jarvis both chuckled and nodded. They shared relieved glances. This was going better than they could have ever hoped!

The queen raised her arms and spoke. Velveeta again translated her message. "Our new freens, Skampersky and Jarvie . . ."

Jarvis winced when he heard the nickname Velveeta had obviously translated to the queen. Bernie chuckled at his discomfort as the queen continued, ". . . will join us for a feast of cheeses and cookies. And while there, they will, because they are our friends, tell us about THE RULES!"

A loud cheer erupted. Bernie felt a little worried about having to delay their return for a feast, but Jarvis couldn't have been happier. Bernie didn't know how long it would take for Kryptos to enact his plan with the giant robots, but if they traveled somewhere close to the amount of time it took for them to reach the moon, then she figured they only had a few days at most.

"Did you hear what she said? Did you hear, B?" said Jarvis.

"I heard, I heard," said Bernie.

"A feast of cookies and cheeses!" Jarvis looked rapturously toward the heavens. Then he suddenly had a panicked look on his face and began patting the pockets all over his jumpsuit. His whiskers fell.

"Kryptos took my Tabasco."

CHAPTER 17

Bernie and Jarvis were ushered to a gigantic building that seemed to be designed out of green glass. The walls glittered and had been polished to mirrorlike perfection. They passed through the arched entrance and walked down a grand hallway lined with rows of holographic portraits that looked like all the monarchs who had come before Queen Madrigal the Magnificent. Hovering above elegant columns, the miniature three-dimensional images of royal alien mice smiled broadly. One particularly broad-chested mouse was wearing futuristic-looking armor and preened his whiskers, curling them constantly with his paw.

The inscriptions beneath the projections were written in the swooping, cryptic language of Velveeta's people and seemed impossible to decipher. That impression changed quickly, however, when Bernie saw to her surprise that, upon staring at the curling script for a moment, the letters rearranged themselves so that she could read them!

King Manchego the Mighty, she read. *Ruler from 3367 to 3399. Under him, the world knew no fear and the Great Peace began.*

Bernie wondered what the *Great Peace* was. Had Velveeta's planet been at war at one point? She found it hard to believe that the friendly little mice could have fought anyone. They were all so cuddly!

At the end of the Hall of Monarchs, they passed through another door into the feasting hall. The room was grand and elegant, and surprisingly comfortable with long tables and cozy green tufted chairs. Soaring green glass columns stretched to a ceiling that was so high up, Bernie couldn't see the top. Bernie and Jarvis were ushered to the front of the room and welcomed to sit in swooping chairs on either side of a throne. They reminded Bernie of tall, curling question marks.

As she sat down on the curved seat, she was surprised to find that artistic creation was also quite cushy. The queen sat in the throne between them and adjusted her long robes. She patted Bernie's paw and, smiling warmly, began chattering to her in the singsong language of her people. She radiated such comfort and warmth that even though Bernie couldn't understand a word, she felt as if she'd known her for years.

Thankfully, Velveeta sat nearby and translated everything. Bernie soon realized that the queen not only wanted to know everything about her, but she also wanted to know everything there was to know about Mice and Dice.

Bernie was no expert and when the conversation moved to the nuances of game play, she turned the conversation over to her best friend. Jarvis was all too happy to explain the finer points of the game play, so Bernie took the opportunity to study more of the alien surroundings.

The room was filled with friendly, chatting, furry green mice. *If I'd only known that this was how aliens really are, it would have spared me many sleepless nights*, she mused. They were just like the mice from back home, except for the fact that they were speaking their foreign language. And, if they were anything like Velveeta, had special, very useful powers.

When the food arrived, Bernie had another reason to revise her thinking. At first glance, the fluffy green cheese dishes and pale green frosted cookies looked unfamiliar. But the moment she put the first bite of cheese in her mouth, her knees went weak and her eyelids fluttered. It was, by far, the best thing she'd ever tasted!

"Where has this been all my life?" she said between large mouthfuls.

"A million miles away on a star you can't even see from

Earth!" said Jarvis. Bernie was surprised to see that, in spite of not having his mini bottle of Tabasco sauce that he always carried, he didn't seem to miss it.

I should learn something from this, Bernie thought. *Just because something is unknown, doesn't mean I should be afraid of it.* She really needed to write that one down. It was something that she was determined to remember as she advanced in the Mouse Watch.

The alien mice devoured Jarvis's explanation of the rules with as much enjoyment as Bernie devoured the feast. His descriptions were accompanied by many "oohs and aahs" from the captive audience. When he was done, the queen stood, her robes swishing against the floor, and the feasting hall went silent. She cleared her throat and began giving orders.

"Zashoop!" she exclaimed.

The dishes were cleaned up and the tables cleared.

Bernie turned to Velveeta and asked, "What's going on, Vel?"

"The queen wishes to play a game of Mice and Dice," he replied.

"What, now?" asked Jarvis between mouthfuls of cookie.

Velveeta nodded. "Then after game, she help you beat bad rats."

Bernie was worried that the longer they stayed, the

more time was slipping away, but she knew that they really had no choice. They had promised to help. She nodded and said, "Okay, then we'd better hurry and get started."

The next thing she and Jarvis knew, they were standing on top of a tall podium that overlooked the massive, grid-like game board outside the palace. Bernie gazed down at the planet surface, still awestruck to see her favorite game come to life. All the little green mice were scurrying around, excitedly preparing to play. She pinched herself, just to make sure that she wasn't dreaming.

I would have never pictured doing this in a million years, she thought.

"Since you are the Game Master," Velveeta said to Jarvis, "you say what we do and where we go."

"Okaaay," said Jarvis. "Um, but I didn't really prepare anything. Usually I've got an adventure written before we do a session."

"How about you do the one we were playing with Juno?" Bernie suggested. "You know, the one with the Rat Zombie overlord?"

"Ah, *No Rest for Ratzenheim the Rabid,* yeah . . ." Jarvis thought for a minute and nodded. "I can do that. Do you think they have a pencil and paper on this planet?"

Almost before Jarvis had finished his question, a green tablet and a stylus were placed into his paws. Jarvis tested the strange writing implement on the tablet and nodded, seemingly pleased that it worked very much like a digital tablet back home.

"Neat," said Jarvis. "Okay, um, Velveeta, can you tell everyone to gather around?"

While Jarvis jotted down some notes to help him remember the storyline of their latest game, Velveeta rushed down the pedestal stairs, loudly calling for all the mice participating in the game to gather around. Everyone, including the queen, then surrounded the base of the pedestal and gazed up at Jarvis with expectant, happy faces. Jarvis finished his notes, then motioned for silence. He lowered his hoodie dramatically and then boomed in a deep storyteller voice:

"Night falls in the twisted woods of Nevermore. You see, atop a craggy hill, the ruins of a tower once held by the evil zombie overlord, Ratzenheim the Rabid. . . ."

He's really good at this, Bernie thought, admiring her friend. Usually, she was the one leading the charge, but it made her happy to see Jarvis in his element, excited and unafraid. At first, she wondered if Velveeta would be able to translate the dramatic scene Jarvis had described, but her jaw dropped as she realized she didn't need to worry.

The landscape began to shimmer and change before them, taking on the appearance of the scene Jarvis described. The sky darkened, and a waxing yellow moon appeared overhead. Dark, twisted trees curled up from the ground like reaching octopus tentacles. Damp, mossy earth appeared at her feet and, in the center of the game board, a hill rose up with a crumbling tower that looked exactly like the one Bernie always pictured in her mind when they played.

How? Bernie wondered, her mouth still hanging open. It all looked so real!

But then she thought about Velveeta's ability to shape-shift and realized that the aliens had more power to affect perception than she'd previously thought possible. It seemed that the same powers he used to understand their language allowed him to connect telepathically to Jarvis's imagination, and bring to life the incredible illusion, one that looked, felt, and even smelled completely real!

Bernie had never seen Jarvis more excited as the Mice and Dice of his imagination sprang to life all around him. He'd loved and lived with the game for so long, Bernie could tell that for him it was a dream come true. His descriptions quickly took on more flourish as the game play commenced, and he waved his arms theatrically as he continued to tell the story.

"The band of weary traveling magicians are startled by the arrival of Ratzenheim's vicious battle troops!"

In response, a group of little alien mice pressed the button at their belts and they immediately shape-shifted into the weary traveling magicians. Just like that, the game had begun. Soon, with the Gem of Twenty Numbers sparkling and flashing in the air as it was thrown, imaginary battles were being fought. Bernie marveled as the group of magic mice in long cloaks and pointed hats took on a very convincing horde of massive, rotting zombie rats!

I doubt that playing Mice and Dice back home will ever be as amazing after seeing this, Bernie thought as she watched a mousemage shoot a level fifty fireball at a hideous zombie, sizzling it where it stood. It was even better than a video game!

At home, a really good game of Mice and Dice could last for days. Bernie, Jarvis, and Juno would play on breaks during the day and at night after dinner. But since they still had to get home from outer space and save the world from Kryptos, Jarvis kept the game short. It wasn't long before they arrived at the triumphant moment when Princess Gorgonzola defeated Lord Ratzenheim with her mystical Staff of Orn. When the rusted crown was seized from the rat overlord's head and he collapsed to his knees begging for mercy, the entire population of the alien planet erupted in cheers.

"Victory to the mousemages!" cried Jarvis. "You all receive chests of golden cheese and three experience points!"

After some more triumphant, happy shouts, the imaginary realm dissolved around them, and all the mice morphed back to their original forms. Jarvis, sweating with exertion from shouting and waving his hands while dramatically describing all that was happening, nearly collapsed.

"Well done!" the queen said, clapping her paws. And when she spoke, Bernie realized that after spending some time together she, like Velveeta, had used her powers to swiftly pick up on the basics of their native Earth tongue. "Now, eet ees time to depart!"

At her command, a fleet of flying saucers rose from behind the green glass palace and landed soundlessly on the surface. Bernie thought the ships looked like glittering silver frisbees—all lined up and ready to commence a rescue mission to Earth.

"My pee-ople arrre ready to . . . *grummbo*, er, accompany you on your mission. You have given us a great geeft, Bernie Skampersky and Jarvis Slinktail. Wee are foreverrr grateful."

Bernie was surprised when the queen then gave her and Jarvis each a warm hug.

Now if only the rest of the mission can go as easily as this part, Bernie murmured. But deep inside, she knew that facing off with Kryptos was bound to be anything but easy. In fact, she knew that they would be lucky if they escaped with their lives and tails intact.

She took a deep breath, reminded herself to think positively, and then she and Jarvis re-boarded Velveeta's ship.

Once inside, Bernie couldn't help still feeling a creeping sense of foreboding. What if they were too late? Would they arrive back on Earth only to find that Kryptos had already executed his diabolical plan and that everything was in ruins?

There was certainly no time to lose.

As the saucer's door closed and Velveeta punched in the coordinates for Earth, Bernie leaned back in her chair and tried her very best to stay calm.

We'll make it in time. We have to!

One hundred alien ships hovered into the air and shot off at warp speed, leaving behind contrails of glowing green light. As the stars melted away, streaming past the saucer windows in long streaks, Bernie hoped beyond hope that everything she was telling herself would turn out to be true.

CHAPTER 18

"The problem is bigger than that," said Jarvis. "We have no idea where Kryptos will launch his attack. It could be anywhere on the planet. You don't even realize how big the R.A.T.S. network is! I was there and I didn't even know Kryptos existed."

"The worst thing would be to tune in to the news and find him attacking some important national monument somewhere," said Bernie. "I just wish there was a way to track him down and stop him beforehand."

An asteroid shot by the window of Velveeta's flying saucer. Bernie watched it fly past, hardly noticing or caring that she was in the vast reaches of space anymore. In the days since she'd left Earth, her fears about it had faded.

There was so much more to worry about.

Velveeta was perched in a small captain's chair, his little

paws dancing over a bunch of different touch screen controls. He paused what he was doing and looked at Bernie.

"What is . . . *track him down?*" asked Velveeta.

"Huh?" asked Bernie. She couldn't quite understand the question.

"*Track.* What is *track?*" asked Velveeta.

"Track. You know, to follow someone," said Bernie.

Velveeta nodded with understanding. "Ah, we say, *gooble.* This means you put a sticky paw on their back when they not looking. We always find our goobles."

"I wish Kryptos was one of your goobles. It would make things a whole lot easier," said Bernie.

Velveeta laughed. Bernie looked at him, feeling confused. "What's so funny?"

"Easy cheesy! Velveeta already gooble Kryptos before he put him in cell. He's a *slorpnut.* A bad rat."

Bernie felt suddenly hopeful. "So you know how to find him?"

"Of course, Bernie Skampersky," said Velveeta. His fingers danced over the lit touch screen and a large map appeared on the overhead display. A red dot was blinking and Bernie knew immediately what it meant.

"Kryptos is in California! And he's right near Mouse Watch HQ!"

She couldn't help wondering if Gadget knew or had

figured out what was going on. Had Kryptos completely fooled her? Wouldn't she be wondering what had happened to them? They hadn't been in communication once since blasting off, and though she had lost all sense of time in space, it felt like they should have been able to complete their mission and return to Earth by now.

"Hiding in plain sight," said Jarvis. "Genius. Typical evil mastermind move."

Bernie moved closer to the map. As she approached, the area around the red dot grew larger and she could see precisely where Kryptos was.

"That's the Hollywood sign!" said Bernie. "And look, the red dot is hovering right over that radio station above it."

"Again, classic evil mastermind move. Seriously, B, we should have figured this out on our own," said Jarvis. "He picks the Hollywood sign, one of the most famous icons in the world, and then cleverly uses a building right behind it to broadcast his evil, fear-spreading propaganda to any gullible rats and tells them that they must join together to defeat all mouse and humankind. Aaagh! Shoulda seen that one coming!" Jarvis slammed his fist into his palm.

"But now we know where he is!" Bernie stared at the map, unable to believe it. She finally felt like they might be able to stop Kryptos. The only trouble was, he was sure to have guards all over the place. She considered calling

Gadget, but remembered again that Kryptos had taken their goggles back on the USS *Mozzarella*.

There was no way to get in touch.

"We gotta break in there, somehow, without being spotted," she muttered.

Bernie paced back and forth in the little cabin, running a frustrated paw through her tall blue hair. There simply had to be a way.

Suddenly, she had it. Wheeling around to Velveeta, she said, "Hey, when your . . . fellows . . . play Mice and Dice, I saw you do something with your belts."

Velveeta nodded and pointed to the belt he wore. "*Dorplebuzz.*" He thought for a minute and then said, "Belt can make wearer any shape. Just press gem and say what you want to be."

Jarvis and Bernie exchanged excited glances. "Velveeta, you wouldn't happen to have two of those that Jarvie and I could borrow, would you?"

Velveeta nodded happily. "Yes, always carry extras on ship. My new freens can have!"

Bernie felt like she'd unlocked a piece of a puzzle that she'd desperately needed to solve. With the help of the belts they could sneak into Kryptos's secret lair unnoticed. Then, after they stole back the Milk Saucer, they could thwart his plan once and for all.

But it might be easier said than done, she thought. And

then, as if to confirm her thought, Velveeta added, "Oh, this is important. Dorplebuzz only last five"—he paused to count on his fingers—"gorzles per use."

"How much time is a gorzle?" asked Bernie, hoping it was a day, or even a week.

"One gorzle equals one . . . minute," Velveeta said. "Quick, quick!"

"One minute? We only have *five minutes?*" Bernie asked, trying not to panic.

"Yes. Bernie Skampersky and Jarvie need to be very quick."

And with a sinking feeling, Bernie felt certain that the little alien had probably just made the biggest understatement in the universe.

CHAPTER 19

"Stay close and remember, we only have five minutes with these." Bernie indicated the alien belts that Velveeta had lent them. Jarvis nodded and the two scaled the brushy hill that led to the fenced-in, abandoned radio station.

The cool air smelled of sagebrush and chapparal. It was one of those perfect Los Angeles nights when the weather was just starting to turn crisp. If she'd been anywhere else, Bernie would have liked to stop and enjoy the stunning vista of Los Angeles from the height of Mt. Lee by the Hollywood sign, but right then all she could think about was trying to get through this mission without a catastrophe.

Velveeta had agreed to stay back at the ship. Bernie had a feeling that if things went badly, there was still a chance that Kryptos might be able to activate his giant rat robots and attack the city below. Velveeta and his incoming fleet were the backup plan.

He's small and mighty, too, Bernie reminded herself. She'd seen what he could do with his mind control and the laser ray on the flying saucer. Plus, only he could communicate with the other aliens that were on their way to Earth.

We just have to do this right. No messing up, thought Bernie. There was no telling what a rat like Kryptos might have up his sleeve. He'd evaded capture and detection by the Mouse Watch for who knew how long. She felt certain that he'd planned for every contingency.

Matching wits with a criminal mastermind wouldn't be easy.

Bernie and Jarvis found a little spot beneath the Cyclone fence that they could just manage, with a bit of pushing and pulling, to get through. Once they emerged within the walls of the station, Bernie wished again that she still had her Watcher goggles. She stared at the cluster of buildings and craned her neck skyward, taking in the strange jumble of towers and radar dishes that rose high into the sky.

"Tony would come in real handy right now," she muttered. So far, she'd never had to do a mission without the help of the enhanced reality provided by Mouse Watch goggles. And without any kind of cell phone, they couldn't call to even alert HQ. For a brief moment she considered trying to come up with some way to signal them, like spelling out SOS with sagebrush and branches, but there was no time. It was up to her and Jarvis to make the best of their eyes, ears, and . . .

"I smell pizza!" whispered Jarvis, his nose twitching in the air. "Oh man, what I wouldn't give for a slice of pepperoni with Tabasco. I haven't had anything to eat since we were on Velveeta's planet."

"I smell it, too," said Bernie. "I think it's coming from that window over there, which means that it's open." She pointed at the largest building and turned to Jarvis. "Okay, can you remember the map that Velveeta showed us in his ship?"

Jarvis tapped the side of his temple. "Yep, it's all up here. We go through the door, make two rights and a left. There's a security station right there. We disable that and then, hopefully, we can find wherever they hid the Milk Saucer without being detected."

"Good," said Bernie. "And we don't activate our belts until—"

"—until we have to." Jarvis finished. "I know, I know. Sheesh, you'd think I was a total noob."

As they sneaked toward the window, Bernie was thankful that they were rodent size and not human. She felt certain that the cameras would have motion detectors, but judging from the remote location there was probably a lot of wildlife in the area and the motion detectors wouldn't be triggered by animals their size.

"Do you see any guards anywhere?" asked Jarvis, peeking over the top of an old soda can.

"I think they're all inside," said Bernie. "Those cameras are all they need to keep watch." She pointed up at a nearby radar dish on the roof.

"Okay, so when we get inside, if I do this . . ." Bernie made a hand gesture, slapping two fingers on her wrist and then pointing them at Jarvis. "You know what to do, right?"

"Um, you order two pizzas and I bring the Tabasco?" asked Jarvis.

"No!" said Bernie. "Will you stop thinking about food? Focus!"

"But I'm starving!" complained Jarvis.

Bernie took hold of his arm and glared up at him. "Okay, listen. If we don't do this right, you'll never eat pizza again, got it?"

Jarvis jerked his sleeve away. "Okay, fine." He smoothed out his jumpsuit sleeve. "So, if you do that hand thingy, it means there's two guards and to watch out."

"Yes, good," said Bernie. "Now, we need a distraction, something to get them to come to the door. I know. . . ."

She bent down and picked up a bottle cap. Keeping low, she sneaked as quickly as she could to the side of the building. Above her was an open window and, conveniently, a long radio tower wire ran down close to it.

The security around here was obviously built without Mouse Watch agents in mind, Bernie thought. She scampered up the wire (something she would have never have been strong enough to do when she'd first entered the Watch) and, using ninjalike agility, swung from the wire and landed on the windowsill in a perfectly executed jump.

The scent of pizza was especially strong. Bernie hoped that the grumbling of her stomach wouldn't alert the guards. She would never admit this to Jarvis, but she was kind of hungry herself. Peeking around the side of the window frame, Bernie peered inside. In front of her was a long, linoleum-covered hallway. At the end of it was a small table with a very round, very preoccupied rat guard that was completely absorbed in his human-size pepperoni pie.

He'd obviously had it delivered.

Bernie took the bottle cap and, winding back, threw it like a Frisbee down the hallway toward a nearby door that led outside. The *clink* and *clang* of the metal cap had the desired effect. At first, Bernie had been worried that nothing could have distracted the guard from his food, but, either because he was a professional or because working for Kryptos made him fear for his life, he got up and went over to investigate.

Perfect, Bernie thought.

She scuttled back down the wire and motioned for Jarvis to follow. She led him to a shadowy spot just outside the door. The big rat guard threw open the door and peered around suspiciously. Thankfully, he didn't think to look in the shadows. As he turned around, Bernie and Jarvis scuttled quickly inside the building before the door slammed shut, and, sticking close to the cinder-block walls, scampered as quickly as they could toward the desk, where they could safely hide.

The guard came back inside, scratching his fuzzy head with a puzzled expression on his face. He marched back to his station and, after climbing up a rope ladder that led to the human-size chair, sat down. Bernie and Jarvis remained hidden by the table leg, unnoticed.

Okay, we go two rights and a left, Bernie thought. She glanced up. The big guard was totally focused on his dinner. Bernie was about to motion for Jarvis to follow her, but when she turned, he wasn't there!

Jarvie?

Bernie glanced around frantically. Where had he gone? From the corner of her eye, she saw a tail hanging down from the tabletop and, with a horrifying sense of dread, realized that he'd been unable to resist the call of his stomach.

"Jarvis! Get down here!" Bernie hissed.

Nothing.

"Jarvis!"

His furry face peeked down. Bernie could tell that one of his cheeks was full.

Get down here, NOW! she silently mouthed.

Jarvis held up a finger in a "one second" gesture. Then, one nail-biting second later, he slid down one of the table legs like a fireman down a pole. When he landed on the ground, Bernie saw that he carried two round slices of pepperoni.

He leaned next to her and whispered, "There were a couple of leftover pieces in the box. I grabbed them when he wasn't looking."

Bernie would have loved to give him a lecture about Mouse Watch agent professionalism right then and there, but instead, she accepted the piece of pepperoni with a grudging thank-you and, munching as she ran, dashed around the corner.

They made two rights and a left without incident. Thankfully, most of the hallways of the abandoned radio station were empty. Bernie knew that looks were deceptive, though. Any one of the metal doors that lined the hallways could have had some kind of nefarious activity going on behind them.

But when they reached the main security desk, Bernie knew right away that they were in trouble. Unlike the hapless pizza eater that they'd found so easy to get past, this security station was well equipped and looked to be state of the art.

It was also completely out of place in the ratty old building. Surrounded by a high-tech, glowing bay of monitors were two rows of beefy-looking R.A.T.S. agents standing at attention. Unlike any of the R.A.T.S. agents she'd encountered before, these guys looked slick and tough. They wore black berets and sunglasses. They had jet-black uniforms with red trim. Their shoes were shined to a mirrorlike gloss.

And they were some of the roughest bunch of animals that Bernie had ever seen. Two of the guards were wart-encrusted horned toads. One was a wiry, tough-looking weasel. Three were rats, and the last one was a creature she'd never encountered before, but had read about online.

A wombat!

With the exception of Jarvis and Juno, the Mouse Watch was mainly composed of mice. It wasn't that they excluded any other creatures, it was just that most small creatures were timid and preferred to hide rather than to fight. One look at the well-equipped station and Bernie knew that their plan needed to be altered. There was no possible way to sneak up on those guards unnoticed.

Thankfully, Bernie and Jarvis were hidden in a shadowy alcove next to a metal bookshelf, so she had a little time to think.

"What should we do?" whispered Jarvis.

"I'm thinking," Bernie whispered back. She bit her thumb, staring at the big monitors. There were more views of the building than she'd ever thought possible. In fact, had she known they would be encountering something like this, she would have been more careful sneaking around outside. Half of the images displayed were infrared. There was a chance that they'd already been spotted and that the R.A.T.S. were just waiting for them to walk into their trap.

An image on one of the monitors caught Bernie's attention. The room that the camera displayed was mostly empty, except for a blazing white glow in the center of it.

"Jarvis," Bernie hissed. "I think I found the Milk Saucer!"

She motioned to the display screen and Jarvis spotted it, too. "Good eye! That's gotta be it. But where is it? That camera could be pointed anywhere."

"Well, I didn't want to do this so soon, but . . ." Bernie laid a paw on the emerald gem on her belt. Jarvis met her glance and knew what it meant. They would have five minutes to convince the guards that they were R.A.T.S. agents, find out where the Milk Saucer was kept, and then break in and get out.

Bernie felt that if they hadn't beaten the odds on their other missions, Jarvis would have probably calculated their chances of success as practically zero.

"Okay, on the count of three," said Bernie

"Wait, what animals should we be?" whispered Jarvis.

Bernie thought a minute. "Mean geckos."

"Really?" asked Jarvis, raising a skeptical eyebrow. "That doesn't sound very ferocious."

Bernie rolled her eyes. They didn't have time to debate this.

"Mean geckos on three," she insisted. "One . . . two . . ."

On *three* they both pressed down on the gem and focused on changing their appearances. Like the Mice and Dice players on Velveeta's planet, their rodent forms blurred for a second and then rematerialized as two geckos decked out in the same berets and uniforms as the R.A.T.S. guards.

"Remember, five minutes!" Bernie whispered.

Jarvis nodded and, as one, the two of them, in gecko form, emerged from the shadows. They marched straight up to the fierce-looking R.A.T.S. guards.

CHAPTER 20

"Halt! State your names and purpose!" said the gruff-looking wombat. Bernie noticed that he spoke with a heavy Australian accent. She had to think quickly.

"Major Slimenose and Captain Stickyfoot reporting for patrol. Kryptos told us to take the post by the you-know-what." Bernie hoped that she sounded convincing.

The guards all exchanged glances. Bernie couldn't tell if they were nervous or skeptical. One of the guards, a toad, leaned forward and said in a deep, croaky voice, "How do we know you know what the you-know-what is?"

Jarvis piped up, "How do we know that you know that we know what the you-know-what is?"

The toad stared blankly back at them and the wombat looked even more irritated than he already was.

"We know what it is," said the wombat defensively.

"We do, too," said Bernie. "And if you keep delaying us, you're going to have Kryptos to deal with." Then, on a bold impulse, she marched right up to the wombat and jammed a finger into his chest. "What's your name and rank? I think he needs to hear about this!"

Doubt flickered in the wombat's eyes. Obviously, Bernie's threat had an effect. After a brief struggle, he waved them past.

"Down the stairs to the underground facility, make a left at the barracks. Second door on the right. You know the code, right? One mistake entering it and you're done for!"

"Of course we know it!" Bernie replied with a snort. But she and Jarvis exchanged quick, nervous glances as they strode down the hall in their awkwardly lanky gecko bodies. A code? Done for? Bernie gulped. Things were getting more dangerous by the second! She estimated they only had about four minutes left before their disguises disappeared. Trying not to appear panicked, she and Jarvis picked up the pace, their gecko feet slapping noisily on the linoleum floor as they walked briskly to the location that the guard had indicated.

Ahead of them was a long flight of human-size stairs that obviously hadn't been a part of the original radio station's design. It looked like they descended to a secret underground area beneath the station. Bernie realized that

Jarvis's instinct about there being a hidden underground part of Kryptos's lair was spot on.

Uh-oh. This might take a while, Bernie thought as she eyed the massive steps.

It took her and Jarvis more time than they'd wanted to make their way downstairs. Their gecko legs were longer than their mouse and rat legs, but not by a lot. And as they got to the bottom, they found that the entire floor was cast in murky darkness. Once again, she wished she had her high-tech goggles. Bernie made her way quickly but carefully forward, feeling the walls to make sure there weren't any hidden traps or holes in the ground. Jarvis followed with equal care.

It's like Mice and Dice but for real, she thought.

In the game they often had to navigate dungeons and keep a lookout for traps. The difference this time was that instead of fictional zombie rats, they might run into real R.A.T.S., which were far more deadly.

After searching a bit, Bernie and Jarvis came around a corner and found a gigantic, gymnasium-size room that seemed to stretch on forever. But instead of a dormitory, the room was filled with hundreds of thousands of R.A.T.S. agents, all dressed for battle. They were lined up at attention as if waiting to be deployed. The sight made Bernie freeze in her tracks even though she knew she was in disguise and they should have recognized her as one of their own.

"What's wrong with them?" Bernie whispered.

"What do you mean?" asked Jarvis.

"Why haven't they noticed us?"

"I don't know but I'm glad," said Jarvis.

But the soldiers were so motionless, Bernie couldn't help risking moving a little closer. There was something curious about them, the way they seemed frozen in place . . . not even blinking!

Her eyes widened when she drew close and realized that they, like the horrifying super soldiers on the moon, were also robots—and they hadn't yet been activated.

Oh no! thought Bernie. *Between those giant mecha-Rats and these robots we'll never stand a chance. There are thousands of them!*

"B, come on!" whispered Jarvis. "None of this will matter if we get the Milk Saucer. He won't be able to activate them without it! We gotta hurry!"

Bernie realized he was right. As scary as the prospect of the army was, it wouldn't be a problem without a power source. Bernie followed Jarvis as the two set off for the door that the guards had indicated would lead to the Milk Saucer room. Bernie's hands felt clammy. She wasn't sure if it was because she was a gecko or if it was because she was so nervous.

Probably both!

The two agents reached the door. Bernie didn't know exactly what kind of security device would be waiting for her when she got there. To her surprise, it was a very simple computer keyboard mounted on a wall next to the metal door.

She and Jarvis looked at it closely. Unlike a typical QWERTY keyboard, this one had the numbers one through twenty-six in sequential order. The two agents exchanged worried glances.

"Tricky," said Jarvis. Then his eyes lit up. "Do you think it's a code?"

"Yeah," agreed Bernie, getting excited. She and Jarvis were great at code breaking. "The numbers represent the alphabet. There are twenty-six letters in the alphabet, and twenty-six numbers on the keypad. We just have to figure out the right code word and then enter the corresponding numbers. But what word do you think it is?"

"We could try 11; 18; 25; 16; 20; 15; 19," suggested Jarvis.

"KRYPTOS?" said Bernie, getting the substitution right away. "That seems way too obvious."

"Well, it could be *anything*!" said Jarvis nervously. "There's no way to crack this! We only have one chance, remember?"

"Yeah, but how do we know that's even true. Can we

trust the word of a R.A.T.S. agent? What if the guard was lying?"

In response, Jarvis pointed up to the ceiling above the door. Two heavy-duty laser cannons were positioned there, pointed directly at them.

"Oookay," said Bernie. "Then let's not find out we've made a mistake the hard way. Gotta think . . ."

Bernie knew that out of all the Watchers, she and Jarvis were the very best at code breaking. They'd solved countless other puzzles before, and it should have helped her confidence with solving this one. However, the more she stared at the keyboard, the more she felt like an answer was eluding her. There were no clues and they were running out of time! Bernie glanced at her watch. Four of their five minutes were gone already!

What am I missing?

What would Kryptos do?

She thought back to her training, when Kryptos had been disguised as Commander Sleekwhisker. What was it he'd said back then? Something about being obvious . . . And then, in a flash she had it.

"It's right in front of our eyes," Bernie said.

"You figured it out?" asked Jarvis eagerly.

"Remember what Sleekwhisker told us? He said, 'The simplest solutions are always the best.' Now that we know it was Kryptos talking, we know that's the way he thinks. This code isn't complicated at all."

She turned to Jarvis, her gecko face split into a wide grin. "Kryptos hid himself in plain sight. That plan worked so well nobody saw it coming. And if I'm right about this—" She glanced down at the keyboard. "The code works the same exact way. It's so simple, nobody would dare try it."

Bernie took a deep, steadying breath. Then, she began to hit the buttons on the keyboard starting with the number one and hitting each number sequentially until she came to the number twenty-six. As she hit the last button, there was a satisfying *click!* and the door swung open.

Jarvis let out a long breath and patted Bernie on the shoulder. "Did I ever tell you that I think you're a genius?"

Bernie grinned up at him. "All the time," she said.

They entered the room and saw the Milk Saucer. It was placed on a pedestal, awaiting Kryptos's activation.

Thankfully, now that's never going to happen, Bernie thought. Relief washed over her from head to toe as she picked up the familiar, warm, glowing object that could change the fate of the entire world and tucked it under her arm. It fit snug and safe against her fur.

Wait. *Fur?* Bernie thought. She looked down and saw that the five minutes that Velveeta's belt had bought them had expired. She was back to her old self and, glancing up, she saw that Jarvis was, too.

"We'd better get out of here," she said. But no sooner had the words left her mouth than a loud alarm began shrieking through the building. Jarvis pointed to the video camera positioned high up on the wall with the steady red light pointing directly down at where they stood.

"They've seen us!" he squeaked.

They dashed out the door and saw two of the R.A.T.S. guards running directly at them. The rats' yellow fangs were bared. Bernie knew at a glance that they were trapped. The guards were sure to have support rushing at them from every direction.

She glanced down at her belt. *If only* . . .

Then she had a very bold idea.

Digital Lasso.

"Quick, Jarvis, your belt!"

She held out her paw. Jarvis didn't question her for a second. He handed her his belt and as Bernie undid her own, she knew that she had only seconds to do what she had in mind.

As she'd expected they would, the rats lunged for the two of them at once. And as they did, Bernie timed her move. All the training she'd had at Mouse Watch HQ on the VR sim and the endless games of Digital Lasso kicked in. The hours of aching muscles as she tried to become faster and faster were about to pay off.

She handed Jarvis the Milk Saucer. Then, moving with lightning speed, she tumbled out of the way of the guards' grasp, and like Houdini doing an escape trick, she whipped the conjoined belts over her head and in a fluid, sweeping motion buckled both belts around the waists of the rat guards. Both rats were so surprised by the unexpected move, they stood there with dumbfounded expressions as they gazed down at the jeweled belts that had suddenly appeared around their middles.

"Hey, who are your number one enemies?" Bernie asked.

Both rats answered automatically. They may have been fierce looking, but Bernie could tell that they were mostly brawn with very little brains.

"The Mouse Watch!" they immediately replied with sneers on both their faces.

And no sooner had they said the name of the mouse agents out loud than their forms shimmered and began to shift. Afterward, both guards stood there, unable to comprehend how they now looked exactly like a couple of small, furry mice wearing Mouse Watch agent jumpsuits.

As Bernie and Jarvis ducked back into the Milk Saucer room, the main force of the R.A.T.S. guards, led by the wombat, came rushing around the corner. Spotting the newly transformed guards, the wombat shouted, "There they are! GET THEM!"

The transformed rats let out two panic-stricken *squeaks* and raced off down the hall with the entire gang of R.A.T.S. on their tails. As they disappeared down the maze of hallways, Bernie flashed Jarvis a triumphant grin.

"Now that was really quick thinking!" said Jarvis.

"Thanks, Jarvie!" Bernie patted the Milk Saucer. "Now let's get this thing out of here and back to Velveeta's ship."

The R.A.T.S. had run back in the direction they'd come from, so Bernie didn't want to risk going that way.

"We need to find another way out. Let's go!"

With the Milk Saucer tucked securely under her arm, Bernie took off. She knew that they still only had five minutes before the disguises would wear off on the R.A.T.S. guards so they needed to get out of there as quickly as possible. When the evil animals found out that they'd been tricked, she wanted to be as far away as possible.

As they raced down the hallway, Bernie spotted a big set of double doors. *That has to be the way out!* she thought.

But no sooner had she and Jarvis crashed through the exit than Bernie realized that she was wrong. Very, very wrong.

They hadn't stumbled through an exit. They had stumbled into the very worst possible scenario!

In the center of a large room was a huge conference table, around which sat a menacing group of animals. There was a massive alligator wearing a fedora. Curled up next to him was a vicious cobra. And, next to them, dressed in an immaculate button-down shirt and pressed khakis, was Kryptos himself.

C.R.O.C.S., S.N.A.K.E.S., and R.A.T.S. With a gulp, Bernie realized they had accidentally interrupted a top-level meeting of the Illumi-rati.

And they were all staring at Bernie and Jarvis.

Kryptos's jaw dropped open. It was an expression that neither of them had ever seen on him before. Kryptos prided himself on always being two steps ahead of his enemies, but, for the first time, he seemed to have been caught off guard.

He glanced down at the Milk Saucer under Bernie's arm and his eyes narrowed dangerously.

Bernie took the cue and, improvising, held out the Milk Saucer like a weapon, pointing it at the assembled villains.

"Nobody move!" she barked. "Hands in the air where I can see them, or I send out an energy pulse from this thing and blow us all to the moon."

The evil leaders drew back in surprise. Then Kryptos seemed to regain his composure. He raised his hands smoothly into the air, and the others followed his example.

"Bernie Skampersky," Kryptos said, shaking his head

with a smile. "You know, I really underestimated you. The truth is, I'm not an unreasonable rat." Bernie kept the Milk Saucer trained on their archenemy as he moved toward them with his hands outstretched. "You've beaten me. You should feel very proud. Nobody has ever done that before. I think you should come and work for me. How about it?"

"Don't move any closer!" she commanded. But Kryptos pretended not to hear. With the fixed, humorless grin on his face, he kept slowly advancing. Bernie could tell that he was calling her bluff, and, the truth was, she had no idea if the Milk Saucer could really be used as a weapon by simply pointing it at someone.

The question was answered for her.

Whether it was because of some magical property the Saucer contained or because it had been designed to tune in to the thoughts of the one who controlled it, Bernie didn't know. But no sooner had Kryptos taken another step when the saucer began to glow with a white-hot intensity.

BOOM!

A blast of energy crackled forth like a lightning bolt, destroying an entire wall of the conference room and revealing the courtyard outside. Rubble cascaded down from the ceiling and the room filled with smoke. Bernie and Jarvis exchanged amazed glances.

Cool! thought Bernie.

Kryptos cowered down, looking panicked for the first

time. Bernie seized her advantage and shouted, "Everybody outside, *NOW! MOVE!*"

Kryptos and the others obeyed immediately. As Bernie and Jarvis marched them outside, she was happy to see that they'd emerged right next to the USS *Mozzarella*. Lined up behind the ship, awaiting activation, were the towering black forms of the giant mecha-rats.

Seeing the *Mozzarella* sitting there, waiting to be launched, gave Bernie an idea.

"Okay, everybody get on the ship. No questions!"

The three Illumi-rati leaders looked scared, but they wordlessly obeyed. Kryptos paused on the ramp, his paws still raised above his head. "You'll never get away with this," he said archly. "My minions will give their lives to take revenge on you."

He pointed a finger at the crowd of R.A.T.S. that had gathered outside the building, drawn there by the sound of the big explosion. Bernie glanced over and saw that there were several hundred of them, holding their weapons at the ready and looking dangerous.

Bernie hesitated. If Kryptos was right, she doubted that she could fire the Milk Saucer enough times to stop them. For a moment, it felt like everything was balanced on the edge of a coin. One mistake and the tides could turn against her and Jarvis. They were only two Mouse Watch agents against hundreds of R.A.T.S.

But then, a loud, vibrating hum filled the air.

Gasps sounded around Bernie as Velveeta's silver saucer appeared behind her and rose into the sky, accompanied by an entire alien fleet. While Bernie and Jarvis were inside finding the Milk Saucer, Velveeta's backup had arrived! A loud, piercing whine filled the air and several green energy beams shot from the fleet of saucers, blasting the ground in front of the R.A.T.S. agents, and carving a massive trench between them and Bernie, at least three hundred feet deep.

Kryptos's army panicked. Screaming like frightened children, they threw down their weapons and begged for mercy.

Bernie glanced up at the flying disks and then back at a very pale, frightened Kryptos. She had a choice to make. Kryptos was the Mouse Watch's number one enemy. What should she do with him?

I need to make the call, thought Bernie. *And I need to make it right now. I hope Gadget will understand.*

She took a deep breath and focused her steeliest gaze on Kryptos.

"Now, I want you to do two simple things," she said. "Number one, when you get inside the USS *Mozzarella* I want you to set the coordinates for the moon. You and your other Illumi-rati dudes are going back to live on that base for good."

"But there's not enough fuel in there to make it back

to the moon!" complained Kryptos. His steely veneer had cracked, and he had been reduced to a pitiful whine. "What if we get stuck in the middle of space?"

Bernie thought about Commander Sleekwhisker's diagram of space and the mysterious question mark that had terrified her down to her bones. She had uncovered the mysteries of space and knew what was out there now. But Kryptos didn't. She smiled.

"That's kind of the point," Bernie said. "In space, no one can hear you squeak."

"Yeah, tough Tabasco," said Jarvis. "You were going to leave us on the moon forever, remember? Consider yourself lucky."

Kryptos regained his composure. Snarling, he said, "If you idiots can find a way back, then so can I. And remember, I, Kryptos, will never forget this. I will make sure you and the entire Mouse Watch pay for what you've done."

"Yeah, yeah," dismissed Jarvis. "Enough with the speeches. What's the second thing, B?"

Bernie smiled, loving Jarvis's newfound bravado. When she'd first met him, he'd been nothing like the tough-sounding rat he was today.

"We want our goggles and watches back," Bernie said.

Kryptos stared daggers at her and then, after stalking inside the Mouse Watch starship followed by the other leaders of the Illumi-rati, tossed out the two pairs of goggles and watches he'd stolen. "Take them!" he hissed.

The door to the ship closed. A minute later, there was a terrific blast as blue jets fired out of the bottom of the capsule. Bernie and Jarvis shielded their eyes as the ship rose steadily into the air, carrying with it the Mouse Watch's archenemies. It was hard to believe that finally, after years and years of fighting, the Mouse Watch would never have to worry about Kryptos and his evil plans again. Without their leader, Bernie felt fairly certain the hundreds of soldiers he'd left behind would be relieved not to have to follow their megalomaniac boss anymore.

But that's probably being way too optimistic, Bernie thought. She'd learned to never let her guard down when it came to the R.A.T.S.

As the ship rose until it looked no bigger than one of the many stars in the night sky, Bernie knew, deep in her heart, that Kryptos would indeed find a way back. She knew that he would try to make good on his threat and would probably bend all his efforts to getting rid of her once and for all.

Let him come, she thought fiercely.

I'll be waiting.

CHAPTER 21

O nce they had their goggles back, Tony was quick to get in touch with Gadget. Under the cover of night, a troop of one thousand Watchers rounded up all the captured R.A.T.S. agents and herded them into flying jails to take back to HQ as prisoners. Bernie used the Milk Saucer to blow up the underground facility, including all the superrobot soldiers and mecha-rats. After that, the fleet of flying saucers evaporated anything else that left even the smallest trace of Kryptos's evil plans.

The Mouse Watch (and their new alien friends) had saved the day, and the entire human world was none the wiser.

Which was how it was supposed to be.

"Velveeta gives his freens . . . er, *friends* . . . a ride back to Mouse Watch?" the little mouse asked.

"We would love that!" Bernie replied.

As they boarded Velveeta's flying saucer, Bernie turned to Jarvis. "So, did you have any doubts?"

"Doubts about what?" he asked.

"Whether we were going to make it. After all, things got pretty hairy back there, didn't they?" Bernie asked.

"Well, *hairy* is a relative term," said Jarvis thoughtfully. "Personally, I enjoyed the part where we got to be mean geckos. It was the least 'hairy' I've ever been!"

Bernie laughed.

As Velveeta's spaceship slowly rose into the sky and shot off toward HQ, she couldn't help feeling proud once more of being part of the greatest organization of heroes on the planet. She'd never again take any of it for granted, either. After spending time facing her worst fears in outer space and on the moon, she felt like she could truly face anything life threw at her.

She felt prouder than she'd ever felt of herself.

Fear is a funny thing, she thought. *The more you confront it, the less scared you feel.*

She made a mental note to write that down in her journal when she got back to her quarters. In fact, the more she thought about her new perspectives and all that she'd been learning while at the Mouse Watch, the idea of possibly writing it all down in a book sounded enticing.

Bernie Skampersky, author, she thought. *Now that has a nice ring to it!*

She resolved to ask Gadget for permission to do just that. But in order to get it published so that humans would read it, she might need some help.

She felt sure that Gadget would know someone, some humans out there that could be trusted.

If so, they'd be amazed to learn about the greatest secret they could ever know—that we've been looking out for them for a long, long time.

As a giant harvest moon rose over the California hills, a long shadow from the alien saucer stretched over a little assembly on the roof of Los Angeles Union Station. Bernie thought about how it seemed so long ago that she'd traveled here from her hometown of Thousand Acorns. Back then she hadn't known a thing about the Mouse Watch; its secret location in the heart of Los Angeles; her best friend, Jarvis; or that one day, she, Bernie, would have made friends with alien beings and defeated the Illumi-rati.

It was hard to believe.

She wished she'd been able to tell that frightened little mouse that one day she would be okay. Back then, Bernie had thought it was her against the world, that she had to prove herself something special in order to give her life meaning and to always show herself fearless no matter what. But now, as she gazed at her alien friends . . . er, *freens* . . . beings that were different and yet so like she was, she realized that the Mouse Watch's message had truly changed her forever. She'd learned to depend on others, that sometimes feeling afraid was okay, and most importantly, that through helping others she didn't need to feel so lonely anymore.

The queen smiled warmly and pulled Bernie into her arms, hugging her gently. "You remind me of my . . . *gooldooby* . . . er . . . ."

And for the first time, Bernie knew what the queen meant without a translator. She knew the word the queen meant because she felt the same about her, too.

". . . your granddaughter?" finished Bernie.

The queen smiled and nodded. "That is the word, Bernie Skampersky. You are forever welcome to visit us. When you do, I will always be sure and have warm cookies and cheese waiting."

"Thank you, Your Majesty," Bernie said, squeezing the kind queen's paws before stepping back. "And thank you for helping us. Your kindness will never be forgotten."

Then Bernie turned to Velveeta, and kneeling down, she gave the only mouse she'd ever met that was smaller than she was a big hug.

"Gloople-boop!" Velveeta said, blushing.

"And thank you for everything," said Bernie softly. "And if you ever need me, just say so. I'd be happy to drop everything and help you."

"Oh, and if you need any help with M and D strategy, you know where to find me," said Jarvis, shaking the little alien's paw.

He grinned and added, "Just make me a crop circle in advance to let me know you're coming. It'll give me time to put together a really great adventure for you."

Both the little green mouse and the queen graciously accepted his offer.

For Bernie, saying good-bye to Velveeta was harder than she would have thought possible. The tiny alien had become a true friend in a very short time and Bernie was definitely sorry to see him go.

"We can't thank you enough, Velveeta," said Bernie.

"Yes," agreed Jarvis. "You saved our lives! If it wasn't for you, we'd still be imprisoned on the moon."

The little green mouse gazed up at her with soft, dark green eyes. "Bernie Skampersky and Jarvie are *friends*. Velveeta thanks you for giving our mice the Gem of Twenty Numbers. Anytime you need Velveeta, just think about him very hard and *BOOM*! He will always be there when you need him."

Bernie felt she still had much to learn about what

Velveeta was capable of. His mental powers had proved to be amazing and she wondered if, in spite of being millions of miles away, his ability to sense others' thoughts could travel that far.

She certainly hoped so.

Bernie gave him one last hug. And then, soon afterward, Bernie and Jarvis were both staring at the sky, trying to pick out Velveeta's ship from among the canopy of a million stars.

"It's so weird that there's a planet up there where they're playing Mice and Dice," said Bernie.

"Yeah," agreed Jarvis. "And I didn't even get to teach them the finer points of Level Ten spellcasting."

"Well, maybe we haven't seen the last of him," said Bernie. "Maybe someday he'll return and join the Watch. Wouldn't Juno be surprised?"

They both chuckled.

"What's the first thing you want to do when we get inside HQ?" asked Bernie.

"Eat as much cheese as I possibly can," said Jarvis. "And make sure and douse it all with as much Tabasco sauce as I can get my paws on."

And Bernie decided that it sounded like a pretty good idea to her, too.

* * *

Gadget Hackwrench presided over the massive assembly of Watchers. They'd all gathered back in the stadium-size conference room. Bernie had a weird sense of déjà vu as she sat down in the exact same place that she, Jarvis, and Juno had sat just days before. The only difference now was that Gadget had personally congratulated her and Jarvis for helping to take down the R.A.T.S. leader. It wasn't exactly the mission they'd been sent to do, and this time, there was no big celebration and no pomp and circumstance. Everyone knew what had happened and everyone was glad that she and Jarvis had made it back in one piece.

Bernie thought back to the conversation she'd had with Gadget just before coming to the stadium.

"It was a mistake," said Gadget. "And I owe you and Jarvis both an apology, I should have chosen the mission leader more carefully. I found the real Sleekwhisker right after you launched. He was on a top secret mission for NASA and had just returned from a trip to Mars." Gadget winced. "Imagine my surprise when my old friend called me up and told me he was recovering in the Bahamas. I can't believe I was tricked. It's my fault for not checking more thoroughly. . . . I . . . I should have seen through his disguise. Kryptos was using our own tech against us. He'd gotten the device from Octavia and fooled me completely."

She sighed and said with a shrug, "I'll have to work on

some new software to help reveal that cloaking program he used."

Bernie thought back to her meeting with the submarine captain and shuddered. Octavia was crafty and it was hard to know which side she was on. She wondered whether the submarine captain had given the tech to Kryptos willingly or if the evil mastermind had stolen it from her.

She gazed up at Gadget and said, "But how could you have known, ma'am? He had us tricked, too. If the signal hadn't stopped working so far out in space and his disguise hadn't flickered like that, we would have never guessed until it was too late."

"I'm just glad the two of you made it back safely," said Gadget. "And make no mistake, eliminating a major base of operations for the R.A.T.S. is a huge accomplishment! You both will, of course, be promoted to Level Three."

Bernie and Jarvis shared happy glances. Level Three meant that there would be all kinds of new, top secret locations that they would have access to within Mouse Watch HQ. It also meant more responsibility, but Bernie was perfectly fine with that.

Now looking down at Gadget on the stage, Bernie was struck again by how much she respected her leader. She hadn't been afraid to apologize when she'd made a mistake and she was quick to own, as the person in charge, anything that went wrong and find a way to correct it. It was a trait that the greatest leaders in history possessed, and it only made Bernie prouder to work for her. One day she hoped to be as good a leader as her hero, Gadget Hackwrench.

Gadget motioned for quiet, and the restless chatter in the stadium died away.

"Thank you, everyone. It's with great pride that I can announce that our mission to reverse global warming has recommenced."

Loud cheers filled the stadium.

"This time, there won't be any . . . er . . . mishaps," Gadget said. "We have a pilot who has generously offered his time to command the new Mouse Watch spaceship, the SS *Gorgonzola*. Will you please give a round of welcoming applause to the one and only, Monterey Jack!"

The whistles, hoots, and thunderous applause threatened to bring the entire stadium crashing down. From offstage, Bernie watched as another of her childhood heroes, a big, barrel-chested mouse with a mustache, emerged, waving and grinning broadly at the assembly.

"It's really him!" she shouted.

"I know!" said Jarvis excitedly. "Can you believe it?"

Bernie was so excited she felt like she would burst. The aged pilot was famous for being part of the Rescue Rangers, the team Gadget had been a part of when she was young. The big mouse gestured offstage, motioning for someone else to come forward. Minutes later, he was joined by Chip and Dale, and it was all Bernie could do to keep from crying happy tears. Seeing the entire group together gave her goose bumps. They had defined the idea of what it meant to be a hero long before the Mouse Watch was ever formed.

They were the ones that had started it all.

The clapping showed no signs of dying down. As Bernie cheered along with the rest of them, she felt happier than she'd felt in her entire life. She had given her life to something she could believe in. She was part of a place where she belonged. Ever since she was little, she had dreamed of being one thing:

A hero.

As she looked at the glowing faces of Jarvis and Juno as they applauded the legends onstage, she realized that she'd been given a greater gift than she'd ever thought possible.

She'd found love. And the friendships she had made would last for her entire life.

It just goes to show you, thought Bernie, *that it pays not to give up on your dreams.* She grinned at Jarvis and he grinned back at her.

Because one day, when you wake up, you might just find that they've all come true.

When the applause finally died down and everyone was hoarse from cheering, Gadget led the entire California

branch of the Mouse Watch in reciting the agent's creed. Bernie's heart nearly burst with pride as she joined the chorus of other voices, saying,

Every part of a watch is important, from the smallest gear on up. For without each part working together, keeping time is impossible. We never sleep. We never fail. We are there for all who call upon us in their time of need. We are the MOUSE WATCH!

EPILOGUE

The wombat, the horned toads, the wiry weasel, and three rats emerged from the rubble beneath the radio station. They'd successfully hidden from the Mouse Watch agents that had rounded up their comrades.

They were highly trained, a better breed of Illumi-rati agents than most.

At least that's what the seven of them believed. And they believed something else, too. That calling themselves "The Seven" had a very nice ring to it. Very sinister indeed.

They also believed that with the disappearance of Kryptos and the other Illumi-rati leaders, someone had to control the criminal underworld. So why shouldn't it be them?

As the creatures made their way out of the stones and

debris, they moved to one untouched building, a simple garage used to house maintenance equipment.

At least that's what everyone, including the invading Mouse Watchers, had thought.

The wombat entered a code on a small keyboard next to the door. A section of the wall slid backward, revealing a staircase that wound down into the darkness. The wombat knew what was down there, knew that up until now, anyone going into this most secret of places without permission would have paid with their lives. Kryptos would have seen to that.

But Kryptos was no longer a problem.

After a glance and a nod at their six comrades, the creatures filed down the forbidden staircase one at a time. Beginning that night, a new terror would be unleashed upon the world. And in the opinion of The Seven, it was a terror of such magnitude and power, nobody, not even Gadget Hackwrench and the Mouse Watch, would ever be able to stop it.

ACKNOWLEDGMENTS

I'd like to acknowledge the entire editorial staff at Disney Hyperion, who have done a fantastic job in helping to make the Mouse Watch series as exciting and wonderful as I'd hoped for it to be. Jocelyn Davies, Kieran Viola, Cassidy Leyendecker, Joann Hill, Samantha Krause, Sharon Krinsky, and Guy Cunningham, you guys are true heroes!

And to my wife, Nancy, thank you for your loving support. You are, and always will be, my greatest adventure.